Love is
a time of enchantment:
in it all days are fair and all fields
green. Youth is blest by it,
old age made benign:
the eyes of love see
roses blooming in December,
and sunshine through rain. Verily
is the time of true-love
a time of enchantment — and
Oh! how eager is woman
to be bewitched!

PIPER'S TUNE

Frances Grove, who has married an American, returns from New York to the village of Overbridge to stay with her brother, Julian. Her object is to see the Coronation and to find a wife for her brother, who is a widower. Her eye falls on attractive Loveday Flayne, who has inherited a cottage in Overbridge and plans to spend the rest of her days in lonely tranquillity. Frances is in no way deterred by the reluctance of Julian and Loveday to marry each other.

Books by Margaret Maddocks
in the Ulverscroft Large Print Series:

REMEMBERED SPRING
THE FROZEN FOUNTAIN

MARGARET MADDOCKS

◆

PIPER'S TUNE

Complete and Unabridged

ULVERSCROFT
Leicester

First published in Great Britain

First Large Print Edition
published June 1994

British Library CIP Data

Maddocks, Margaret
    Piper's tune.—Large print ed.—
    Ulverscroft large print series: romance
    I. Title
    823.914 [F]

ISBN 0–7089–3097–2

Published by
F. A. Thorpe (Publishing) Ltd.
Anstey, Leicestershire
Set by Words & Graphics Ltd.
Anstey, Leicestershire
Printed and bound in Great Britain by
T. J. Press (Padstow) Ltd., Padstow, Cornwall

This book is printed on acid-free paper

For
Kathie, Peggy and Anne

1

The Exile

THE letter from England lay amongst the others, slim, insignificant, but unmistakable against its American fellows. Discarding the thick envelopes, curiously uniform in their size and handwriting, Frances picked out Julian's thin scrawl, hung her fur coat in the closet and began to read the flimsy sheets before she had stepped out of her overshoes. The warmth of her apartment, after the crisp cold of early winter in New York, vanished as always when she had a letter from home. She felt the thieving draughts of her brother's study and she saw the clouds blowing up against Spedding Hill and heard the rain spattering the west window. She smelt crumpets by the fire and she could picture it all in the kind glow of firelight, logs from the copse (Julian said they had cut it this year) and she almost felt her face burn as she toasted the crumpets.

And then she came to the end of the letter:

The family send love,
Your loving brother, as always,
Julian.

It was twelve years since Frances had brought Peggy Twyford to America to spend the war with friends in Massachusetts. In nineteen thirty-nine Peggy's parents, frantic in the safety of India, had asked her to take their child across the Atlantic. She had not then known that Landon Grove would meet her off the boat, fall in love with transatlantic speed and marry her before nineteen forty was fairly born. There were moments when she regretted her hasty marriage, but they were few and passed. Gradually she had come to accept and avoid the inevitable deadlocks, which arise when two different nationalities fail to understand each other's fundamental characteristics, and on the whole she had been happy. There was a bad time when she longed to get back to

England and do something personal about the war, but the arrival of her daughter in nineteen forty-two took up her life and energies. Roberta was now ten and led the untrammelled existence of American youth, with a light veneer of British politeness — an attractive mixture. Frances's parents were dead and her brother Julian was the only tie which pulled her back to England, a country which gradually faded into a cosy and comfortable memory.

She had never returned.

As the letter fell back into its original folds and lay quietly under her hand, an unfamiliar sadness swept over her. With a start she thought: 'I am homesick.'

"Will an orchid do for tonight?" asked Landon. "I forgot to ask what you were wearing."

"My black frock, I think," Frances answered. "Thank you, sweet. An orchid will do beautifully."

"I got two. They're in the icebox."

"Bless you."

"Kid all right?"

"She's over at Flannagan's. I said I'd fetch her in about half an hour. I had a letter from Julian."

"Oh! Everything O.K.?"

She knew his interest was kindly though insincere, but she had to tell him about the letter. She had to tell someone.

"Marcy is getting married."

"Really? Good for Marcy. I always forget exactly who she is."

"Goodness, Landon. You must know about Marcy. She's Father's youngest sister and she's only a year or two older than Julian, which would make her just over fifty. She came to look after the children when Judy died and it's an absolute tragedy for them to lose her. Julian sounds distracted. He says — listen — he says:

We are dumbfounded, as I am sure you will be to find that Marcy is in the throes of love and is being married in March to one Jack Lowesmore of Molesworth. The idea is that she keeps an eye on us from Molesworth and we manage with A Woman. But Molesworth is six miles off and there are only two buses a day, so she might

4

as well be going to darkest Africa. No one in Overbridge has ever heard of anyone in Molesworth and she would never have met Jack Lowesmore if he hadn't come over to buy pigs at Crombie's and broken down at our very door. The Hand of Fate undoubtedly. I am going to see if Ann will come home later on and look after us. Johnny is still a weedy little wretch and there must be someone to fuss him a bit.

She paused:

"Oh, and then there's a bit more, nothing of interest." Her eye ran over:
I wish you'd come some time soon, dear sister. It seems a long time since we saw you.

Julian always called her 'dear sister' at least once in his letters. It was a remnant of a family joke and the 'dear', slightly emphasized, often meant the reverse, but it warmed Frances and again her heart was split open a little with tenderness for all things past and half-forgotten, their fierce affection for each other all through their unsteady childhood, the early death

5

of their parents and then her escape.

She gave a sigh, half nostalgia, half relief.

"I can't imagine living in England any more," she said.

"That's a pity," said Landon, "because that's what we're going to have to do for three months."

"Landon! What are you talking about?"

"What I say. Someren is sending someone to England for a few months and he says it can be me if I like because of my English wife. We could be there for the Coronation. What do you say?"

She sat back, her round dark eyes bright with surprise.

"I can't believe it. But what about Roberta?"

"She comes too. Someren says we can all go by plane. He thinks you may be useful for contacts and entertaining. It won't be all play, you know. I've got to fix up the new contracts and get things through a lot of ministries and you'll have to help."

"Of course I will. Oh darling, how wonderful. When?"

"Early spring."

She would have liked to have slipped on to the floor at his feet but in the past two years her figure had thickened and although she was not fat (or so she deluded herself), crumpling bonelessly on to the floor was not for her. She took a breath held in her diaphragm as was her habit at intervals during the day, and then smiled gaily at her husband. Her skin was as clear as when she left England, but her dark hair had turned grey early and last month she had reached the landmark of having a blue rinse.

"I shall have to be in London most of the time and perhaps go to Belgium and Holland, but we could spend some time at your brother's," Landon went on with his slow drawl.

Suddenly Frances saw him at Overbridge, cold, impatient, complaining about everything from the coffee to the warm beer.

"You can't possibly come to Julian's."

"Why not?"

"You'd hate it."

"I should not. I was in England before

7

the war and I was crazy about it. I'm very fond of England. That's why I married you. You know it."

He had often told her that the unhurried calm and integrity which he considered typically British were her chief charms.

"Landon, dear. You know nothing about England. I mean *my* England. You simply know it from the inside of the Savoy, and before the war at that. You'd be miserable at Julian's. There's no central heating and the draughts would kill you."

"But it will be spring before we leave. You've always raved about your English springs."

"So I have, but they can be horribly cold. We'll acclimatize ourselves by turning down the heating for the next few weeks."

He gave a shudder. "Do you want me to freeze to death?"

"Not yet. You can do that when we get to Julian's. I must write to him right away."

★ ★ ★

8

Julian Lenham was surprised to receive a reply so soon for Frances wrote to him regularly only on the first of the month.

"Can I have the stamp?" said Johnny.

"May I have the stamp, please," said Julian, nagging gently.

Johnny said nothing.

Julian looked at his son over his glasses. Was he going to have asthma again, or was he just being — ?

Johnny sighed deeply and as he sighed he wheezed. Julian tore the American stamp off his sister's letter.

"May I have the stamp, please," he repeated. Marcy said he had to be firm. He smiled at his son, thinking it was all rather ridiculous.

Johnny looked at his father and suddenly smiled back. "Please," he said, "and may I? Now can I have the stamp?"

He wheezed again, took the scrap of paper and lay on the hearthrug with his stamp album. He thought with sudden horror that it was going to happen again. He wasn't going to be able to breathe. He began to pray swiftly to himself. The

Lord's Prayer right through, thinking about every word. It sometimes made a difference.

"All right, old chap?" asked his father.

Johnny nodded, breathing manfully. He was nine and he had had asthma ever since his mother died.

"Blast," he said quietly.

His father looked at him sharply, ready to chide.

"All right, then, only bother, but I've got this one. It's the same as last time."

He gave another uneasy breath.

"It'll do to swap."

Julian began to read the letter.

... *so I shall come over in the spring and bring Roberta and see the Coronation and maybe stay on a while. Could we stay with you, at any rate for part of the time? I could perhaps help you out a little after Marcy goes until you find someone else. I hope Johnny is better ...*

The letter rustled thinly, as Julian looked into the heart of the fire.

10

He thought of the close companionship of their childhood, for they had come home from India together to go to school and had spent their holidays with various relations. When their parents had died in an aeroplane accident they were already orphaned by time and distance and the tragic drama of it passed over them. They continued to drift from aunt to aunt until Julian qualified as a chartered accountant. He began to practice with an uncle's firm in Hinwood and on coming into control of his small capital at the age of twenty-one he set up house on his own with Frances as an intermittent housekeeper. She worked at intervals, typing for the doctor, driving old Mrs. Lake's ancient Daimler, helping at the Frale kennels. They had been very close in those days, reflected Julian, living separate but intimate lives. Nothing had ever been so carefree before or since as those years before the Second Word War.

It had all come to an end when he married.

In his mind his marriage was vaguely mixed up with imperial crowns and the sweet high notes of trumpets, for he had gone to London for the Coronation of George the Sixth and had there met Judy. She was three years older than he was, divorced, with one child, Ann, then a year old.

His battery of aunts and uncles thought he was sorry for her, but this was not so. No one could be sorry for Judy. He was quite simply, from the moment he set eyes upon her, in a state of bemused enslavement. He married with all his wits, to say nothing of his relations, telling him he was making a mistake. Fortunately no one knew enough to say: 'I told you so.' No one knew that Judy's temper was hard and sharp except Frances, for Judy quarrelled speedily with Frances, and she escaped thankfully to America, and Judy's unfaithfulness lay always like a secret stone in Julian's heart. But Judy was dead, killed by a bomb while Julian was in Italy in nineteen forty-four. He had come home on compassionate leave to deal with Ann, aged eight, and a delicate, querulous baby son.

Judy had never liked Friar's House,

where Julian and Frances had lived, but she had stayed there after the war began, to be safe from the air raids. Ludicrous to think that she had been killed by a stray bomb in a safe area. Julian grimaced to think that she would have said it was his fault. He had tried to be sorry she was dead and there were moments, if Johnny's asthma tormented him or Ann had a tantrum, when he missed her strength and there were odd spaces of time when he longed for her body, but he never felt the loss of her kindness. For she had never been kind. Gay, witty, forceful, but unfailingly malicious, that was Judy. No, he was not sorry she was dead.

Marcy came in to lay the supper, which they now ate in a corner of the study to save fuel. She was a tall woman, overweight and cheerful. Though she was fifty-three and had never been a beauty there was an attraction about her which made people say that Jack Lowesmore was a lucky man. In the months before her wedding she became full of last rites and admonitions.

"I will make the marmalade," she said.

"It should see you through and if you're careful with the bottled fruit — "

"Look, Marcy," interrupted Julian, "tell all this to Ann when she comes, will you? I don't care and I shan't remember."

"Well, you'll just have to manage somehow. Mrs. Herbage will come a bit more, she says. I suppose I ought to feel wicked to leave you, but I don't."

Marcy looked with a practised eye at the table to see what was missing. She had kept house and done most of the work for Julian for the past eight years. She had nursed him through jaundice. She had sat up many nights with Johnny and she had administered the only corporal punishment Ann had ever known. Her marriage brought the world at Friar's House to a stop. Beyond The Day no one really expected life to go on.

"Frances says she may come over in the spring," said Julian.

"Oh, that'll be nice. I hope she brings some of that tinned ham she sent last Christmas."

14

"Don't you ever think of anything but food?"

"Hardly ever. Now and then I give Jack a thought."

She gave a convulsive laugh, hearty like a man's.

"Johnny, bed," she went on, subsiding suddenly to graver things.

Johnny rolled over on his back in front of the fire and wheezed gently, while Julian and March exchange looks.

"Like your spray?" Julian asked his son.

"Not yet," said Johnny. He could feel the weight gathering on his chest. Slowly he got up and went to the door, going with an unnatural lack of complaint which was ominous.

"Shall I come and help you into bed," asked Marcy.

"No," said Johnny shortly.

No one rebuked him. The unspoken 'Thank-you' lay in the air.

"All right. Leave the door open."

Julian knew that he would be lucky if he spent an undisturbed night, though at each attack he was astounded at the calm bravery of his small son. He became like

15

an old man, fighting for his breath with system, knowing what to do, resenting help and sympathy.

'Devilish complaint,' thought Julian and picked up his sister's letter again.

2

The Travellers

THE six-ten local waited patiently in the bay of Hinwood Junction for the arrival of the London train. The guard was having a cup of tea in the porters' room and the engine driver was leaning out of his cab, surveying the scene as if all his life lay in front of him before he proceeded to Appleford, Frale Halt and Overbridge. The bay did not seem to belong to the hurry of the London train and the few people who used the six-ten knew each other at least by sight. In the air there was the pleasurable sharpness of the sea ten miles away and dusk draped the hills.

Ann Forstal stroked the nose of a cocker puppy and wondered what her stepfather, Julian Lenham, would say when he saw it. There were already two rabbits, five hens, a dog and an expectant cat at Friar's House, but

17

when Robin brought her the puppy she had been unable to refuse. There was something about Robin's devoted eyes which reminded her of the spaniel. It was gratifying to be loved by Robin and the way he went drooling round, so lovelorn that he could not work and hardly ate, made her feel a little like Helen of Troy and Cleopatra combined, but if only Henry behaved like that, everything would be wonderful. She allowed herself the luxury of five minutes thought of Henry. Normally she was more self-controlled, for even at eighteen she realized that thinking of Henry was a waste of time. As the train slipped down the cutting of the lime pits she let her thoughts drift round Henry's careless compliments and her self-esteem rose. It was a good thing he had gone to the West Indies because if he had still been in London, the appeals of her stepfather would have brought a less dutiful response. But her grandmother had not been as broad-minded as usual about Henry and Ann was not sorry to escape from her tiresome warnings.

She came back from a trance where

Henry was gently running his lips up and down her arm, to look at the eyes of Robin in her new dog's face. The woman in the opposite corner smiled at her.

"How old is he?" she asked.

"It's a she," answered Ann.

"They're always more affectionate."

"So they say. She's not three months old yet, or house-trained or anything."

She had a moment of misgiving about the welcome her new pet might receive.

"She's called Tinker," she said.

The woman smiled again. She had a face which broke easily into a half-smile and made her look as if she found everything in life faintly amusing. Above her head was a neat array of good luggage. She wore a well-cut suit the colour of milky coffee and a duck egg blue shirt which matched her curiously light eyes.

Ann wondered who she was as she began to gather together her suitcases and her dog and her tent-like coat, for there was only one more station and that was Overbridge. The other passenger made similar motions with her own things.

19

"Shall I help you with the dog?" she offered.

They both found themselves on the platform of Overbridge, which was deserted except for a small group at the far end talking to the stationmaster. This separated into its component parts of Johnny, Julian and young Bentley from the garage, and while they all joyously greeted Ann, and the stationmaster extracted her ticket from her, and Julian explained that the car had broken down and young Bentley would be driving them, and young Bentley made a movement as if he might in time lift a suitcase, Loveday Flayne surveyed the scene bleakly, with her luggage neatly round her feet.

'If you go to live in the country,' Janet had said, 'you'll be a foreigner for ten years at least at your age.'

Loveday was beginning to be tired of people who said 'at your age', as if forty-four automatically made one more sensible and less vulnerable. But perhaps Janet had been right about the ten alien years ahead. Loveday sighed and then found that a tow-haired boy had taken

20

her bags and wanted to know if she had a car.

"No," said Loveday. "I thought perhaps I could telephone for a taxi. Is there a box?"

"There's a phone in the office. You can use that," said the boy. "You'll have to pay threepence though."

He looked at Loveday as if he thought she might not have so much. "And it won't be any use for a bit," he went on, "because young Bentley is just going with the Lenhams and old Bentley is laid up with one of his bad turns and the new chap on the Lower Road charges double at night. Tell you what though. I'll just go and catch young Bentley before they start."

He dashed off and again Loveday was alone on the station. It was now too dark to see far but somewhere up in the wooded fringe round the hills was her new home. This was her station, across the yard she saw the sharp squat spire of the parish church, her church, and somewhere in the cluster of stone houses was her grocer and her butcher. Overbridge was now her village. She

21

swelled with possession and the feeling of loneliness ebbed.

Young Bentley left his fares struggling with Tinker and asked Loveday where she wanted to go.

"It's a house called Crafers up over the hill. Do you know it?"

"Oh yes, of course," said young Bentley reassuringly, and his words brought the house out of its lost obscurity. "Old Miss Cox lived there and she died and — " he looked at Loveday with new interest. "You going to live there?"

"Yes," said Loveday faintly.

"Well, I've got the big car. You might as well come up with Mr. Lenham. I've only got to drop them in the village."

"Won't they mind?"

Young Bentley gave a cross between a sniff and a snort to indicate that it would be all the same if they did, and, apologizing profusely, Loveday found herself sitting next to a small boy and being walked over once more by Tinker.

"Bentley always packs us in like this. He'll charge us both full fare and save his costs. If you say a word he makes ominous threats of leaving you to the profiteer on the Lower Road."

"I've already been warned about him."

"By Ernie? How the poor devil makes a living I don't know. No one approves of him. He's new."

Julian laughed pleasantly.

"I'm new too," confessed Loveday. "Are the natives hostile?"

"Not all of them. But you have to take us as we are and love us. We dislike being criticized. If you go around saying there never was anywhere as nice as Overbridge — "

"Well, there isn't," asserted Johnny.

"You see?"

"Here we are," cried the girl. "Now you will have some room."

"You will be glad to be rid of us," said Julian.

Loveday could not see his face properly in the dark and she thought with a dart of regret: 'I shouldn't know him again.' She could not even see the house clearly except that it was by the church. She watched the door open and a rectangle of light swallowed them all, the boy, the girl, the dog and the stooping man. A fat woman met them on the mat and shut the door as young Bentley handed in the last of the suitcases. The car proceeded over the hill and down a wooded lane. At the end was Crafers, solid in the darkness, an owl hooted as Loveday stumbled up the path. There was no hint of the view.

'I must buy a torch,' she thought as she paid young Bentley

She had never lit a paraffin lamp in her life and as she now did so after many fumblings and blackened fingers she thought with relief that she had a permit to wire the place for electricity and build a bathroom. It had seemed simple enough in London to say to people: 'No, it's all rather primitive, but I can picnic there until it's done. The spring is coming and it's so peaceful. I shall have nothing to do but get the place in order.' In practice, she found that the effort required to boil the kettle on an oil stove which flared and roared and went out under her inexperienced hand was such, that by the time she was drinking tea she had no energy left to cook any supper. For the first

24

time since she had decided to come to Crafers she was filled with misgivings. A fog was coming up over the valley and although she was above it she felt cut off from the world. Even the lights from the village below were blotted out.

'I won't start the fire,' she said to herself. 'I will just unpack and go to bed.'

Yet even that involved the filling of a hot-water bottle and a new onslaught on the oil stove. She went up the narrow staircase carrying her suitcases one by one. The light of six candles which she placed in a row on the mantelpiece flickered round the shadows and mice scurried in the walls.

★ ★ ★

In the morning it was raining. Loveday lay and watched it sweep across the valley like an approaching cobweb and then she lay and listened to its gentle spattering and thought how peaceful it was. That was before she discovered that owing to a slope in the yard, a small river had flowed under the back door. But as she lay in bed and looked out on the drenched landscape, she refused to be daunted even by the thought of the oil stove. She had escaped from her life in London in search of Peace and here it was enveloping her, soothing her. How wrong all her friends had been when they foretold boredom and mental stagnation. Such things were impossible when she was confronted with this vista, rain-sodden though it was. Loveday heard a cock crow far down in the valley and the plaintive bleat of a lamb. From her window there was not a house to be seen, but from the back of the house there was a vignette of the village, the spire of the church amongst the grey stone houses. It was fringed on two sides by the boughs of oak trees in the middle distance, like the chapter heading of a book on the country.

Loveday's father had left her the cottage amongst his other assets, complete with a non-paying tenant, who had once been his nurse. In the autumn she had died and Loveday had come down to Overbridge for the first time in her life to see about selling it. On a bright

October day, with the small garden full of michaelmas daisies and dahlias, with here and there a freak primrose or a lupin, valiantly blooming from a season before, she had fallen in love with it. She decided not to sell and thought vaguely that it might do for her old age.

That was before the invasion. In November Alan, her brother, Diana, his wife, and his small son had arrived from Persia to stay at her house in Kensington until they found a flat. And they had not found a flat. From the moment at the end of the war when Loveday's father had died and left her the thin house in Kensington and a degree of independence it had never been really empty. There was Aunty Flo who came for a week, had a stroke and then took almost as long in dying as King Charles. There were school friends who came up from the country to go to theatres and Women's Institute meetings at the Albert Hall and who brought friends or children or a husband. There were the babies Loveday minded for a week while their parents did the sights and the Festival Year, thought Loveday gazing at the damp patch on the bedroom ceiling, had really been, as the girl had said in the train about most things, 'The End'. For, amongst other people, a distant aunt from the Orkneys had turned up and a long lost and extremely dull cousin from Australia. It wasn't until her brother and his family arrived that she suddenly became weary of them all. At first, in her new-found freedom from the tyranny of the kind despot who had been her father, she had enjoyed her popularity. That was before she realized that most of her visitors, if not all of them, came because it was a convenient hotel and it was free. It had given her a shock when she had accidentally heard Diana say to Alan in that high voice of hers which Loveday found so wearying: 'But anyway, darling, it's cheap.' She had shut her ears quickly, hating what she had heard, torturing herself needlessly by imagining what her brother might have replied.

Just before Christmas there was an offer for Crafers. The agents and her solicitor advised her to take it. To let it at the restricted rent allowed by law would be uneconomic, they said. *You must realize*, they wrote, *that it is not a particularly desireable property.*

And then, sitting amidst the debris of breakfast, she had decided that it was desirable to her. She and no other would live at Crafers. She would be able to take her fill again of being alone. To her that was desirable indeed.

"Alan," she said carelessly, pouring out more coffee. "If I go and live in the country would you like to live here?"

"Where would you go?"

"Never mind. I'm asking, would you?"

"Yes," said Diana, answering for her husband. "It would be wonderful."

"You want to let me the place?" said Alan.

"You could have it rent free if you'd pay the rates and keep it in repair."

And so it had been settled, not then and there but gradually, with much talking it over and arranging and signing of documents and opposition from the family solicitor, until in the end Loveday began to think that her friends were right when they said she was 'quite mad'.

Ellen Cox's furniture was still at Crafers. When she died she had left it, having apparently no relations, to her nurseling or his heirs. No one wanted it, least of all Loveday, but it was there, tidy and well cared for, if by now somewhat dusty. There were blankets and bedlinen and pots and pans and an unknown friend of Ellen's had, at Loveday's request, lit a fire twice a week and kept the damp at bay. If Loveday liked she could move in and sort things out as she went along. There were certain treasures from the Kensington home which she wished to take with her, her desk, a Regency breakfast table which had been her great grandmother's, some miniatures, her mother's tea service, books; it became a longish list and another thing about which to argue, for Loveday had always felt guilty that her father should have left her the lion's share. She knew Diana resented the fact, though Alan bore her no grudge, knowing that nothing could repay the years she had given up in looking after her parents. Yet the treasures which he would gladly have taken from Loveday, the spinet, the china dogs and the scrap screen from their nursery, were just the very objects which brought forth scorn from his wife. It was arranged that a room at the top of the house should be regarded as Loveday's, if and when she wanted a few days in London.

It had been unnecessarily exhausting, thought Loveday, in Miss Cox's bed at Crafers, longing for her early cup of tea but hating the idea of getting it. She had a week in which to organize the cottage and parley with the builder about electricity and the bathroom, dispose of Ellen's furniture and arrange for her own to refill the gaps. Or so she thought. It seemed a long enough time. She had nothing to do but please herself, a sensation so novel as to be doubly pleasurable.

She let her feet dangle from Ellen's high bed, until they found the rag rug and her bedroom slippers. The washstand, momentarily useful, would have to go, and the Edwardian dressing-table of yellow maple, the texts, the picture of a coy lady in becoming draperies, sighing at her departing lover, and the Goss ornaments. But the chest of drawers, in early Victorian faded mahogany, was good, thought Loveday, appreciating its simple lines and the sheen on its drawer knobs. The week ahead of her shrank into an inadequate slice of time. She hurried down the stairs anxious to begin.

★ ★ ★

As the door had closed at Friar's House on the evening of Ann's return Julian had said of Loveday: "I wonder who that was?"

"That woman? I picked her up in the train. She was rather nice about Tinker. Had been pretty once," said Ann, seeing Loveday's far-off enchanting youth and killing it stonedead. "Quite forty, I should say."

"Oh," said Julian. He was forty-seven himself and took mild pleasure in the obvious fact that the younger generation regarded him as a 'slipper'd Pantaloon'. Still, he straightened his shoulders and thought, as he did occasionally, that he'd like to have his hands on a pretty woman again, or just a woman. He looked at Ann and was suddenly frightened at what a man might do to her. She looked so gay and fresh in spite of her gash of lipstick and the absurd wisps of her urchin cut and her curved slenderness hidden in the tent-like coat. She had all her mother's looks and her grim common sense, but her father, who was in South Africa and who made his presence felt only occasionally by food parcels or a whimsical letter, had evidently endowed her with an unexpected softness. It was a bewitching combination and Julian wished sometimes that he could lock her up until she was safely married.

Marcy brought in the supper and told them all to hurry or it would get cold. From the hearth rug Ann and Johnny looked up hot and tousled from a loving scramble with Tinker, while Lob, the displaced setter, growled with jealousy from his basket in the corner. The new dog was accepted without much protest. Marcy was leaving so soon that she did not care and Julian's heart was always lost to anything small.

"I've brought a new record. You'll love it, Daddy. Marcy, I've got you a wedding present, an extra one. I hope you'll like it. It broke me even though I made it. I'll go and get it."

"Finish your supper," said Marcy ungratefully.

"No, you've simply got to see it."

She was gone and back again with a froth of pink on her arm.

"It's nylon," she said, and added: "Outsize."

Marcy's eyes opened in her round face and her two chins melted into her thick neck as she laughed the hearty chuckle of the fat woman.

"It's indecent," was all she said, "and I should catch my death of cold."

Julian took the *Financial Times* to his chair by the fire and put on his glasses and pretended he saw nothing of this.

They were holding up the nightdress and laughing, two women against all the men in the world.

"Jack'll love it," said Ann. Marcy went on laughing. "Tell me about everything, Marcy. What are you going to wear? Where are you going for the honeymoon? What are you — "

Johnny slipped off his chair and lay at his father's feet stroking Tinker. 'When Ann comes home,' he thought, 'they talk such a lot. Everywhere you go there are women's voices, at the sink, in the bedrooms, round the fire, drowning Ted Ray and Twenty Questions.' He leaned against his father's legs and suddenly caught his eyes in sympathy. His breath came comfortably, so that he did not know he was breathing and his thoughts chased on without the panic interruptions of wondering how to fill his lungs.

I shall be thankful, wrote Julian to Frances, *when Jack has made an honest woman of Marcy. Ann says would you like to come a week earlier so as to be here for the festivities. I don't recommend it and I'm sure it would bore Landon, whom I look forward to meeting.*

Julian added the last sentence out of politeness. In effect he could not believe in Landon and was liable when writing to Frances to forget his existence. The child was easier to picture. She would be horrible, of course, all American children were, it was said, and he was one of the many Englishmen who generalized with great confidence about a diverse people of whom he had but the slightest acquaintance. His pen ran on:

Ann has just arrived. I don't think she really likes living with her grand-mother and she doesn't know what she wants to do. She's a great responsibility and if I didn't sleep like a log I'd be awake half the night worrying about her, if you know what I mean . . .

He stopped as he heard the clinking of teacups. In any house which held Marcy there was permanent tea. When tea was rationed she had shamelessly borrowed from her neighbours and mortgaged herself as long in advance as her grocer would allow. There was nothing, she often said, that she wouldn't do for a quarter of a pound of tea. Moaning distractedly all day that she could never get through her work, she stopped at two-hourly intervals to prepare, brew and drink tea and then wash up the results, a time and motion study which often made Julian shudder.

3

The Return

JULIAN had not been able to meet Frances, and he had only spoken to her on the telephone, both of them inhibited by absence and almost shy, but recognizing each other's voices with the first breath, Frances eagerly emphatic and Julian gruff and hesitant.

The excitement of Marcy's marriage and departure, combined with the preparations for the arrival of his sister and her family, had made life so hideous for Julian for some weeks now that when both events were imminent he began to wonder how he could face either.

"Don't forget they'll be here by four," warned Marcy.

"As if I could," muttered Julian. "Where's Ann?"

"Sleeping it off," said Johnny through his porridge. "She didn't get in until three. I heard her."

"Never tell tales of that sort, young man, especially with your mouth full. Wait till you have to creep up the stairs. Three, eh? That's rather late. Where had she been?"

"A whole lot of them went to a dance at Newfold," said Marcy comfortably. "Tony Gregg took her. Don't look so disapproving. You know about it. She's very pretty."

"I know," said Julian. "That's the trouble. I wonder sometimes whether I ought to lock her up. What were they doing until three o'clock?"

"Oh, ask me," said Marcy. "What do you think? What did you do?" she laughed.

There was a comfortable vulgarity about Marcy's laugh which Julian would have enjoyed if it had applied to anyone but Ann. He looked back at his own youth through a mist. 'Marcy's no good at bringing Ann up, and nor is her grandmother,' he thought. Startling pictures of Ann bringing babies home in the cold snow ran across his eyes. Did all parents have such misgivings? He had no one to ask. It was a time when, if he did not miss Judy, he wished there were someone else in her place. And there had been no one. It seemed as if Judy had drained him not only of passion and desire, but of all liking for women, for when he met a woman, before he had finished saying 'How do you do' he wondered where she hid her claws.

Ann now appeared in a red housecoat, tousled and unbathed, but enchanting. With a sink of the heart Julian realized that once more they were going to talk about the wedding and, hastily gulping the last of his coffee, he fled to a cheerless attic where he spent the rest of the morning making Marcy some bookshelves. He was clever at carpentry and used it like a drug. In the past half-dozen years much longing, bad temper and worry had resolved themselves into a great deal of miscellaneous woodwork in various parts of the house, from farm animals for Johnny to an unsteady standard lamp in his study.

* * *

From the moment Frances arrived in England she felt personally responsible to Landon for the weather.

"You'd think it never rained in the States at all," she said angrily as Roberta whined and Landon shivered. "I think it's rather soothing."

"I prefer to have my nerves jangling and keep dry," said Landon, impatient at the delay on the part of the commissionaire of the Grantchester Hotel in producing a taxi.

They all had bad colds and Landon began to bleat about what he called 'his sinuses' as if all the world but he were born without them. Frances sneezed and blew her nose and trusted in the future, while Roberta developed an alarming cough, which she produced and developed if she thought anyone was looking.

The parks, which Frances had pictured gay with flowers, Londoners lolling happily on the grassy sward, tickling each other under the chins with buttercups or sleeping in the sun, were sodden wastes, a study of greens and dismal shades of beige. Nothing seemed to make up for the weather, not even a glimpse of the new young Queen, not even, thought Frances, a decent cup of tea at last. She was sick of their moanings. 'Dear God,' she found herself praying, as she knelt for a brief moment in St. Paul's, 'please make the sun shine.'

She took Roberta to see the sad ruins of the City and to the Tower of London and Westminster Abbey. The Changing of the Guard moved Frances almost more than the pageantry of her country's history, but Roberta became tired and missed her funnies and Landon was interested in all these feudal survivals but unmoved. She realized with disappointment that she must enjoy her special pleasures by herself.

She had an inconsequent idea that at Overbridge the sun would be shining and when Landon suggested leaving London on the following Saturday for a week's vacation before he started his work proper, she agreed with all the ardour of a child promised a visit to the circus. The fascinating uncertainty of English weather rewarded her, and after a week of grey, drizzling days, London suddenly appeared newborn and rainwashed and bathed in shy sunlight, which made everyone say cheerfully: 'Lovely day.'

It was late afternoon when they arrived at Overbridge. The London office had lent them a car, which at once cheered Landon almost as much as the sunshine, and Frances realized that one of the drawbacks to the past week was the fact that they had all forgotten how to walk. When the signposts began to say 'Overbridge' Frances felt at home. She was certain that the moment she arrived at Julian's house any care she might have would slough off like a snakeskin. That, however, was before she realized that they were lost.

"For Pete's sake, Frances, you must know where we are," said Landon exasperated.

"I tell you I don't," wailed Frances, all her decision and efficiency momentarily gone.

"But we can't be more than five miles from the place. Here's another signpost. 'Trenthouse 2 miles.' Where's that?"

"Over Spedding way, I think," she answered, trying to remember a place where she and Julian had once gone in a bygone age to play in a tennis tournament.

"Do you mean to tell me," said Landon in amazed fury, "that you've never heard of a place not five miles from your own home?"

"Of course I've heard of it. I just don't remember."

She realized that she didn't remember many things and when they eventually stopped to ask she was struck by the strangeness of Landon. She had been married to him all these years and here he was in the middle of England, an obvious alien, asking the way in a Boston accent which she had always found so attractively English and which now sounded harshly foreign.

"Mother," said Roberta. "It's pretty, isn't it? So cute and small."

Frances was looking at an unfamiliar white monument at the crossroad, which turned out to be a new filling station, and a settlement of grey boxes where she had been planning to show her husband the view. It was the Overbridge Housing Estate.

"You go straight up the village and it's the stone house on the corner by the church," she said in a small voice.

★ ★ ★

Loveday had come into Overbridge to buy herself another paraffin stove and interview the builder. She had enjoyed the walk after being tied to the house while settling in and now she stood in the quiet street feeling lost, aware that passers-by were giving her an interested but unfriendly stare. At the house on the corner there appeared to be a certain amount of excitement and she turned unashamedly to watch. A car drove up and disgorged a well-dressed woman in grey, a child in a curious hat and a large man, assured looking, wide in the hips and bespectacled, with a hat and tie which had not been bought in England. Out of the house spilled a small boy, a dog, a girl with a high laugh, a fat woman and a tall, thin, sandy-haired man.

'Why, I know them,' thought Loveday. 'They gave me a lift the night I came.'

Above the heads of the visitors and

44

their luggage she saw the girl's face break into recognition.

"Hallo," she said, with the brief friendliness of her generation.

"Good afternoon," said Loveday, who disliked 'Hallo' as a greeting, and then thought that perhaps she sounded stuffy, so she added: "How's Tinker?"

"Fine, thank you," said the girl, picking up a rawhide suitcase with a graceful lunge and vanishing after her visitors into the house with a wave and a smile.

'The young are much nicer than we were,' thought Loveday, turning her mind to paraffin stoves. She had had little contact with people of Ann's age, for her friends' children were mostly still at school and her own youth, between the wars, seemed a long way off.

The peace which she had so coveted once more enveloped the street and she shut out the thought that she was lonely.

4

New Faces

LOVEDAY found that the builder who had said he would put in her bath was elusive. She had as yet no telephone and after she had more than once walked a quarter of a mile in the rain to the box on the main road, she was put out to hear a female voice retort that 'Mr Gorman warn't there and she didn't know when he would be.' After some days of this, Loveday pursued him shamelessly and at last found him at the top of a ladder dealing with the roof of the school, a shocking building consisting of one room and two sinister outside conveniences. From within piping voices recited their twice times.

"Mr. Gorman?" said Loveday.

Mr. Gorman looked down enquiringly at Loveday from a great height and before the conversation ended she had a crick in her neck.

"About my bathroom, Mr. Gorman. The electricity is in the house now, the men came yesterday. What about my bathroom?"

"Ah!" said Mr. Gorman, his position giving his words an Olympian force. "With any luck, I'll start on Monday week."

"But that's another ten days," moaned Loveday.

"Can't help it if people die," answered Mr. Gorman, "and this muggy weather die they will. Can't stop 'em."

Loveday was puzzled over what effect the death-rate might have on her bathroom, but when her eyes fell on a notice-board propped up by the school gate: 'Gorman and Son, Builders and Undertakers', everything became clear.

She hoped Mr. Gorman would have luck.

At a brisk pace she started back up the hill, telling herself she liked a good walk and looking forward to the view at the bend where she could see Crafers snug against the woods with the valley at its feet. Her garden was small but a few yards from the back door was a twenty-acre field on which lambs were now frisking. Every time Loveday looked at it she told herself how right she was to leave London.

The sky clouded over, so she did not linger on the hill and by the time she had reached the top and had turned into the wooded lane, she was wishing she had a car. The view, however, was always worth the long climb.

She had walked round the house and opened the back door, when she was aware that a dark shape lay between her and the frisking lambs. Horror-struck, she saw that a few feet from her hedge and as many yards from her window was a caravan. Beside the caravan was an old car, recently painted bright red by the hand of an amateur. Loveday observed that smoke was proceeding from the chimney of the caravan, which was, she reflected, more than it was doing from her own.

She put her key in the lock. There were sounds behind her back and a voice said; "I've been waiting for you to come home."

She swung round and saw what in

the half-light she took to be a boy. He was wearing dungarees and some sort of flying-jacket. He was also very dirty. Her first impulse was to ignore him, but he produced a bucket and smiled so widely that his teeth showed white and even across his smudged face.

"I only want some water," he said. His voice had a twang that was not quite cockney. "Mrs. Livers said she'd let me have some, but I thought you'd be nearer. Shall I come round?"

"What are you doing in the field?" said Loveday severely.

"Living here."

"Living?"

"Yes, mayn't I live?"

Loveday found that he was laughing at her and she disliked it.

"Mr. Livers has given me permission. I like the view. I did not imagine you would mind."

"I like the view too, and now when I'm in the kitchen I shan't see it," said Loveday shortly. "There's a tap in the yard. You can fill your bucket there."

"No, thank you," said the young man suddenly. "I'll go down to the farm."

He walked slowly into the dusk as if he was tired and from the back he no longer looked like a boy. She wanted to run after him, beg him to take all the water he wanted, but she stood rooted to her doorstep, hearing the clank of his bucket as he went slowly down the steep slope towards the farm.

She was in the right. She couldn't have strange dirty young men invading her privacy, spoiling her view and, for all she knew, hitting her over the head. She went into the house and was glad that she could now turn on the radio and pretend she was not lonely.

★ ★ ★

Rising late after a restless night Loveday looked out of the window and saw that the caravan had moved now into the far corner of the field, where a little tongue of grass ate into a small clearing of the wood.

'He won't have any view at all from there,' she thought with something near remorse.

There was a noise something like a

commando raid and the red car lurched across the field, out of the gate, down the lane and was gone.

★ ★ ★

The milkman was in the habit of delivering a pint bottle at the double, the paper boy threw *The Times* more or less in the direction of the house from the gate, but the postmen (there were two, Loveday discovered, who worked alternate weeks) were always ready for a few words. Without the postmen Loveday would scarcely have spoken to anyone. She christened them 'High' and 'Low'.

High, when asked, promised to find someone who would come and give her a hand in the house and that was how she met Mrs. Spracker. It was from her that Loveday eventually learnt everything she wanted to know and a great deal she did not, for Mrs. Spracker talked.

"It is not," said Mrs. Spracker, scrubbing the kitchen table with the entire contents of a tin of Vim, "that I'm a gossip. I don't hold with gossip, but you can't help hearing, can you?"

"Seen the young man in the caravan yet? Works for Livers, Dad says." Mrs. Spracker always spoke of her husband as if he were a universal father. "Been ill, Dad says. Not much use, Dad doesn't think. Seen the Vicar? He means well. Married my Dolly real lovely he did, but o' course he ain't liked by everybody. Stands to reason. Mrs. Livers asked me about you last week. I told 'er I was 'elping you, so I daresay she'll pop along. I put in a word for you."

Mrs. Spracker really launched Loveday into society, for Mrs. Livers, while not actually calling, spoke to Loveday in the lane and asked her if she wanted to join the Women's Institute.

"Well, it's very kind," said Loveday. "I've only just come and I hadn't thought."

She was happily ignorant about the function of this admirable body and not at all sure she wanted to join anything which might disturb her peace.

"Second Thursday," said Mrs. Livers, as if announcing a duchess's at-home day. "You have to be proposed and seconded, of course."

"Do I?" said Loveday. It was now beginning to sound like an exclusive club. She wondered if she might be black-balled.

"At half-past two," went on Mrs. Livers. "Jeff brings us back in the jeep, so you won't have to walk up."

Loveday wasn't sure whether she was committed to join the Women's Institute or not, but she gave Mrs. Livers her soft, charming smile and said everyone was so kind, thinking privately that she would forget all about it for the moment.

She reckoned without Mrs. Spracker, for although, through her, Loveday gradually gathered a mine of slightly inaccurate data about the inhabitants of Overbridge, she had no idea that Mrs. Spracker was spreading all she could glean about her employer. She could, had Loveday realized it, have damned her with a sentence and a half, but Loveday was lavish with cups of tea, gave her two of Miss Cox's old carpets and the wash-hand stand and Mrs. Spracker thought she was a lovely lady and said so. The glances which Loveday now received, when she went to the village, were kindly, though curious, without being as yet friendly, and the day after the caravan appeared the Vicar called.

Loveday was in the garden, wondering how she would ever know a weed from a plant. The Vicar advised her to join the Gardening Society, which met every month at the Duke's Head. He, it seemed, was the President.

"I'm sorry I haven't been to church," began Loveday.

"Oh, that's all right," said the Vicar. "No one ever does. I'm used to it, but its rather sad. I just christen and marry and bury!"

He looked like a bedraggled blackbird, as he took off his cycling clips and followed Loveday into the house. With an exhausted air, he sank unasked into a chair, clicking the clips like castanets.

"I'm sorry that my wife isn't with me, but she doesn't really have time to call and that sort of thing, you know. We have three children. Keeps us very busy. And we have bees and a pig, and of course hens, and then there are the parishioners." He added them almost as an afterthought.

"Mothers' Meetings and so on?" answered Loveday.

"Yes — yes, exactly so. It's a full life."

"Would you like some tea?" asked Loveday. "I've got electricity now and after a month of paraffin I feel as if it is magic."

The vicar brightened and said he would, and as the ground floor only consisted of a small kitchen with a living room leading from it, he was able to keep up a flow of conversation through the door. This he did in a series of gasps and Loveday felt if the kettle did not speedily boil he would die at her feet.

"You know young Peter Colefield, I daresay?" he asked, as Loveday took down the Spode cups and saucers and wished she had remembered to clean the silver teapot.

"I don't think so, I don't know anybody."

"He said he had spoken to you."

"Oh?"

"He is living at the moment in a caravan in Livers' field. He spoke to you, I believe, the night he came."

55

"Oh!" said Loveday again. She felt exposed before the Vicar as an uncharitable Pharisee who refused a glass of water.

The Vicar looked sideways over his glasses and laughed. "I gather he startled you. This is Spode, isn't it? Are you interested in china?"

"I'm sorry if I wasn't very helpful, but you know, there he was, bang in the middle of my view, and — "

"Yes, my wife told him he was unwise to park so near to your hedge, but he's a thoughtless creature, not stupid, you know, but thoughtless. My brother is a parson in Yorkshire, and he wrote to me about him. He was up there to begin with, Colefield I mean, but found it too cold. He had been ill. He was in Malaya, you know, and some terrorist potted at him, not seriously, I believe, but then he had dysentery and finally he came home. He has bought a caravan and is going to help the Livers for some hours a day and write a book about Malaya in the evenings. I'm sure I don't know — "

The Vicar suddenly began to drink his tea while adjusting his cycling clips.

"Choir practice," he said, "and I have to feed the hens. My wife has gone to Hinwood to the Ruridecanal Conference. It was luckily on Tuesday. She can do the shopping and she will get some of Blore's sausages. Tuesday, it is the only day Miss Slape can baby-sit. Do you know Blores? Just behind the church — wonderful sausages — "

Loveday had the feeling that he was settling bedraggled feathers, as he wound a long, rusty, black scarf round his neck twice, crammed on an unclerical hat and lurched off wildly on his bicycle. All his movements bespoke great weariness. The wind caught the ends of his scarf as he turned the corner.

'Anyway, it's downhill for him all the way home,' thought Loveday thankfully. Other people's exhaustion always brought on a feeling of tiredness. She wanted to be tired with them — for them. She wanted to do their job and save their energies. It was the reason she had never had a life of her own. It had indeed lost her a husband.

She could have married many times, for she had had, in youth, an enchanting sparkle, and in maturity a lively sympathy which men found attractive. She had also clear eyes, dark curly hair, a figure which went in and out in the right places and a candid, cheerful expression. When she was young she had more admiration than was good for her. She paid dearly for breaking men's hearts — only temporarily, as it turned out, for they later consoled themselves, with the exception of one who became an embittered bachelor in the Congo. Fate had punished her by letting her fall in love with Anthony Flexford.

It was all over now. Nothing remained of those horrible few years but an emptiness of the heart. Anthony had been happily married, with two children and a successful career as a barrister. At the end of the war his wife, who was a friend of Loveday's, had a violent and transitory affair with an American and Anthony had turned to Loveday for help and comfort. It was almost inevitable that they should fall in love, and they did, with a thoroughness which frightened them both. Then Virginia had returned and for the sake of the children Anthony had taken her back, but the passion for Loveday had remained and had gone on sapping their energies and distorting their lives with its conflicts. Loveday had suffered for both of them. When divorce was discussed it was she who had pointed out exactly what Anthony would be losing. When his work suffered she wore herself out with worry and in the end they suddenly stopped loving each other, until they were not even friends — and the bleakness of this discovery was to Loveday more agonizing than those other years of desperate surreptitious loving.

If her cousin Joan's children had not come up for the pantomime and all developed measles, a situation with which Loveday had to deal, she thought ruefully that she might have had a nervous breakdown. But there had been no time and now, two years later, here she was at Crafers, heart whole and fancy free. It was a wonderful feeling. She washed up the tea things and fetched her fork from the garden and thought how restful it was to have a space for her thoughts.

The brown and green of the landscape were like a painting. There was even

Corot's inevitable touch of red in the distant splash of Peter Colefield's car, intruding in the dusk.

★ ★ ★

Mr. Gorman came and knocked a hole in Loveday's kitchen wall, and a lavatory pan, a bath and a wash-hand basin lay about brazenly in her front garden. A crisp wind blew through the aperture, plaster disintegrated into everything and the peak of discomfort was reached when the water was turned off without warning, leaving Loveday yearning like a traveller in the desert for tea.

She had bought some literature on gardens and was walking round the rose bushes, book in hand, wondering where she would find an 'outward bud' to prune as instructed, when she saw the light-haired boy walking up from Livers with his buckets. She wished he would bring her some water, but after what had passed she could hardly ask him. Thorns tore at her ungloved hands and the wind whipped her ears.

"I say, Miss Flayne," said a voice,

"Aren't you doing that rather early?"

She straightened her back with a half-suppressed groan, for it ached unaccountably, and blew a strand of hair out of her eye, to see the light-haired boy.

"The book says — " began Loveday defensively. It was queer how irritating she found this creature.

"Well — I shouldn't go on till the beginning of next month — not up here. I'll show you how when the time comes," he added with affable superiority.

Loveday could not bring herself to thank him. He was maddening, standing there with his broad, unquenchable grin. It was impossible to snub him. Suddenly the wish to do so passed and Loveday smiled back, the lazy soft smile of hers, half-tender, half-laughing.

"I wondered if you'd like some tea — actually," he said.

"Good heavens, wouldn't I? The water has been turned off for hours and they never warned me so I haven't a drop."

"Yes, I know."

"How on earth?"

"Mrs. Spracker told her Jeff and he

told Mr. Livers and he told me."

"How amazing."

"Not really, haven't you ever lived in the country before?"

"No, at least not real country, only the tidied-up part full of stockbrokers. Do you mind if I'm filthy?"

"Not a bit. It will make a nice change. The Vicar says I frightened you that first night and I wanted to come and apologize, only you were so frosty. You see I'd been mending the tractor and I couldn't wash until I had some water and you wouldn't give me any."

He opened her gate and she walked with him across the field.

"Churlish, wasn't I?" she said.

"Very. Not a bit like Sir Philip Sidney."

He grinned again. He had a wide mouth and good even teeth but his face was thin and creased into sharp lines when he smiled. He was so much taller than she was that he had to bend a little to look at her, and it gave him a protective air.

"It isn't quite finished," he said, opening the door of his home and disclosing a compact design of drawers and seats and boxes. "I'm making the most of the fitments, but I shall have to get some help with the curtains."

Loveday could have bitten her tongue off when she said with her automatic but often so regretted kindness: "I could machine them for you."

Her own curtains were still not entirely finished and she repeatedly told herself that for at least a year she was going to do absolutely nothing for anybody else.

"That's kind, but Mrs. Livers will do them, I think."

A contrary quirk to her nature made her instantly disappointed that someone else also had kind impulses, but she merely said: "Oh, well," and looked through the lozenge of a window at the view.

For in spite of hiding his home in this corner by the wood he still had his share of the view, a small composition of trees in a line etched, leafless, on the skyline; in the corner of it was her own roof and the gay green of her new water butt.

Behind her the Calor gas roared and speedily boiled the kettle and soon she had washed her hands at the sink hidden by a flap in the corner and was sitting on a cushioned seat with a large mug of tea in her hand, while her host was fitting a record of *Swan Lake* on to his gramophone.

"Do you mind being here alone?" she asked.

"No, do you?"

"I? Oh, being at Crafers? No, I'm thankful. I was sick of being eternally cluttered up with people."

"So was I."

"But you're so young. You ought to like people."

"Well, you're young too, the same thing applies."

"But I'm not young," she laughed and suddenly wished it were not so. Normally she made no secret of her age, but something kept her from saying: 'I'm forty-four.' She hesitated, but only said: "I'm older than I look."

"Maybe, so am I."

He did not pursue the subject, it was, reflected Loveday, unimportant; the crescendo of the music filled the small space. He flung himself about ridiculously as if he were conducting. In the interval of turning the record he asked: "What's your name?"

"But you know, Flayne."

"I meant your Christian name."

"Oh," Loveday hesitated. She came of a generation which did not begin with Christian and advance through friendship to a surname.

"Loveday," she said. It sounded for the first time significant and not ridiculous. "I was called after my grandmother," she added apologetically.

"But it's heavenly," he said, turning round swiftly so that his bright eyes looked straight into hers. He repeated it: "Loveday," he said, then again: "Loveday."

He did not ask if he could call her by this name but from that moment he used it often: 'I say, Loveday, listen to this.' Or: 'Loveday, do you like ballet?' 'Loveday, can you ride?' It was almost as if he enjoyed using it and by the time he took her home, escorting her gallantly to her front door, barking his shins on the brazen lavatory pan by the bath, giggling with vulgar appreciation of its obscene appearance, Loveday felt she had known him for years. When she went to bed and saw the light of his caravan like a golden eye across the meadow, she was for the first time glad he was there.

5

Frances Lectures

"**Y**OU'LL just have to marry again, Julian," said Frances, sitting with both feet in the fender, a screen at her back and a small near-mink cape round her shoulders, for the spring temperatures were not what she had pictured. Landon was in London and Marcy was honeymooning. Ann was at a rehearsal of the local Dramatic Club. Roberta and Johnny were playing Corinthian bagatelle and presumably freezing to death in the dining-room.

Julian poured out two sherries.

"I couldn't — there isn't anybody."

"Nonsense," said Frances, "I shall find someone — suitable, of course, and you'll just have to marry her. I know you think I'm joking, and of course I am, but it would be a solution, Julian dear. Can't you think of anyone?"

"Nobody at all, except old Miss Rawson. What about her?"

"No darling, seriously. What are you going to do? I simply shan't go back until something is settled. You can't keep Ann at home indefinitely. It would ruin the girl's chances."

"I don't see why. She seems quite happy."

"Just now because we're here and there's a lot going on, but I've been talking to Marcy. My dear, we must find you someone."

"There were all those harpies who answered the advertisement for a housekeeper. Surely one of them would have done."

"They all of them wanted to fiddle about doing the flowers and must have help with the rough, and no cooking. I never saw such a mob. And they'd all have married you."

"Not all of them, surely. First you say I must get married and then you complain when five very dull women present themselves."

"They wouldn't have been a scrap of good. But seriously, darling, don't you ever want to marry again — or something?"

"Or something, perhaps, but I was rather put off marriage. I — I wasn't exactly blissful, you know, except for the first six weeks, and even that was exhausting."

"It isn't always like that." Frances contemplated her own happiness with the smug lack of understanding of all happily married people.

"Maybe not." Julian poured out another sherry.

"I shall find someone," said Frances gaily, "see if I don't."

"Much better confine your energies to finding someone 'for the rough'," said Julian.

A happy banging from the next room marked a certain lack of restraint on the part of Johnny and Roberta.

"He's better anyway," said Frances.

"It's that horrible child of yours."

"She's not horrible and she's getting such a high-hat English accent I'll never dare take her home. I wish I didn't have to live so far off."

"Yes, so do I."

It was refreshing, thought Julian, to have someone charming and vital in the house who was ready to organize everything, from Johnny's asthma to a prospective bride.

"You know," said Frances, stroking her sleek hair and stretching her be-nyloned legs into the fender, "this is the sort of thing I'm always homesick for."

"What?"

"This. Firelight, sherry out of grandmother's decanter, and the carpet just a bit shabby."

"A bit? Marcy says it's in holes."

"So it is — but you know everything back home is so, I don't know, sort of glossy. If ever I get really poor I shall come back here."

"Thanks awfully, you needn't bother. I shall be much too poor myself to keep you."

"Hateful brother. But you know it doesn't seem to matter so much here what you have and haven't got. There's a kind of elegance in life."

"Rubbish. You know quite well you have never ceased to grumble about the cold and the kitchen ever since you came.

Elegance indeed. Have another sherry?"

"Oh, don't think I don't adore the States, but there are things you miss."

"I'm relieved to hear it."

"You know Landon is simply sold on England. Honest!"

"I don't believe it."

There was a noise outside like the murder of the little princes, and Ann came in followed by a young man with a beard, a middle-aged woman and several nondescript looking girls with their hair hidden in scarves.

"I say, Daddy, Aunty Fran, we can rehearse in the play room, can't we? We all trailed down to the back room at the Hall. Ogle had forgotten to tell us library night had been changed and so, there we were, and Miss Lavington has come all the way in from Upper Spedding."

No one waited for any answer. Friar's House was well known and everyone except Miss Lavington knew the tortuous way up the back stairs and across the older parts of the house.

"I'll take the electric fire from Aunty Fran's room. You won't mind, will you?"

Frances shivered. She was now resigned

to a permanent state which was just chilly enough to be uncomfortable, but not really cold enough to complain.

Miss Lavington, who had once cherished a longing to go on the stage but had no other qualifications, was the producer. She put on her glasses and tried to sort out the mob.

"I think," she said diffidently, "we'd better just read Act One tonight and see how we get on. Joan, perhaps you'd read in Mrs. Lambe's part, she said she wouldn't be able to come to the first two rehearsals because they had just killed their pig. Now then, Mr. Shaw, you're our male lead, and Ann, you're going to try Sally, aren't you?"

"I say, Jimmy, you simply must shave off that beard," said Ann.

Joan and Jane said they liked beards. Ann said they were horrible. The two girls from Chisholm's General Stores looked at each other without speaking, and Miss Lavington said 'Quiet, please,' without much effect. Miss Otway then discovered that she had left her copy of the play at home and could she share with Ann? Ann suddenly remembered that she hadn't fetched the electric fire from Frances's room and departed to fetch it. Johnny and Roberta having heard of the excitement followed her in through the door, and ignored all orders to go away.

It was surprising that they did manage to read as far as the end of Act One, but goaded by Miss Lavington's gentle voice the two girls from Chisholm's Stores found their breath, putting hasty and nervous emphasis on to the wrong words, and, with the quenchless hope of all village drama societies, they arranged a rehearsal for the following Tuesday.

Ann thought, if only Marcy hadn't gone and married there would have been some coffee, but the prospect of standing about in the cold kitchen and washing up afterwards restrained her hospitality. She did miss Marcy and Aunt Fran wasn't a great deal of help because she organized so.

★ ★ ★

On the second Thursday of the month two-thirds of the female population of

Overbridge made their way to the Parish Hall for the monthly meeting of the Women's Institute. Mrs. Lowesmore, otherwise Marcy, who was now an outcast at Molesworth, came over on the bus to see her old friends and have lunch at Friar's House. Only Frances was at home, Johnny being at school and Roberta having gone to the Vicarage to spend the day. As Marcy walked into the long passage she saw, through the study door, Frances clutching the telephone with one hand and clawing coils of hair in agitation with the other. Marcy edged by into the study and tried to look as if she were not listening to the squawks which Frances was making, surprise giving her voice an increased American inflection.

"Oh — I couldn't — not possibly, I don't know how — Well, if I must, if you really think so, perhaps I could, only I'll be awful — half past two — yes — yes — yes — Mrs. Livers — goodbye."

She hung up the telephone and appeared with a hunted expression.

"I can't think how it happened, but I've promised someone called Livers to speak at the Women'a Institute on 'Domestic Life in the United States'."

"I thought we were going to have a demonstration on Rag Doll making."

"So you were, but someone broke her leg and Mrs. Livers is trying to get a substitute. She said, rather oddly I thought, that if the worst came to the worst, would I speak."

Frances began to laugh.

"Isn't it awful?"

Marcy filled her old chair and her chins began to shake as she laughed.

"Well, you can tell them all about your washing machine and your washer-upper and your superior coffee and your deep freeze, they won't be half as bored as we are."

Frances began to look less alarmed. What one might and might not say ran through her mind as she entertained Marcy and told her that Johnny was better and that Landon was coming for the week-end. Ann had taken the car to Hinwood to buy a new dress and to go to the movies.

"I wish Julian would marry," said Frances over an early lunch. "Someone suitable, of course; surely there's someone who would do. Marcy, you must know someone."

"My dear, every spinster in the village would marry him tomorrow if he'd ask them, but he's frightened of them all, and anyhow none of them would be any good."

"Then we must go farther afield and find someone. Honestly, Marcy, if we all really try it could be done."

"You want everything so fast, my dear. You always did, that's why you like the States."

"If I see something that wants fixing, I fix it," said Frances, screwing the knob on the coffee pot as if Julian's marriage was a simple thing which could easily be accomplished by hanging up 'Do It Now' in poker work. "It's ridiculous to say that it can't be done."

"Haven't you thought that he might be utterly miserable? I have an idea he was before, you know."

"He wouldn't be if we managed it properly. You see."

Frances spoke as if nothing remained but to buy the ring and Marcy remembered that she had a trick of getting what she wanted.

"It will probably sort itself out and Ann will stay, anyway for a time," she said comfortably.

"But she's wasted down here and I've got another scheme for Ann, I want to take her back with me."

Marcy opened her mouth to speak and then shut it again. She did not agree with anything Frances had said but as usual she found it too much trouble to argue.

"I'll wash up," she said, "and you can make a few notes of what you have to say."

Frances was beginning to see herself now in her new role as speaker and she stood opposite the mirror practising an opening sentence.

"I'll wear my lemon and grey tweed."

She knew that whatever she wore she would probably be the best-dressed woman there and the thought raised her spirits.

At two o'clock Marcy said she must go because she was one of the hostesses, and by urging Frances not to be frightened

77

and also not to be late she succeeded in reducing that poor woman to a state of nerves which even the lemon and grey tweed hardly dispelled.

At the parish hall Marcy removed the key from behind a special stone by the porch — a hiding-place well known for generations to all Overbridge — and let herself into the fustiness of the back room. As usual she was the first, and she began to fill and light the urn, a temperamental gadget, prone to a variety of mishaps. In the hall itself a kitchen table displayed signs of business, such as a bell and a box and glass of water, and facing it were between forty and fifty unyielding empty chairs; on one side of the hall was a cheerfully roaring stove, and on the other side another stove, unlit unless an extra shilling was paid and this was only done after due thought in extreme cold.

Mrs. Livers was the next arrival and with her she brought a reluctant Loveday, who had been promised a lift back in the jeep. She was introduced sketchily by Mrs. Livers, and, feeling that the whole thing was faintly masonic after peeping into the hall and seeing the chairs, she asked Marcy if there was anything she could do.

"No, unless you like to put out some cups and saucers. The other hostesses haven't arrived, as usual. They are meant to come early."

"She can't do that," protested Mrs. Livers, "she's a visitor." But Loveday was already clattering happily amongst the cups and saucers and telling Marcy that she lived at Crafers and loved it.

"At least I shall when Mr. Gorman, has my bathroom finished," she added.

"I can sympathize if you have Gorman, though really he's no worse than most and he does work well when he does it, which is a change these days."

Women of all shapes and sizes flowed in a friendly stream through the back room into the hall; Marcy, arranging buns and cossetting the urn, knew everyone. Many asked her how she enjoyed her honeymoon and how the Lenhams were managing and Loveday, all ears, and realizing that she had shared the Lenhams's taxi on her first day, tried to make the various scenes into one picture and failed. By the time Frances arrived the Hall was nearly full, except for the few who came on the only bus from Pladging, which arrived inconsiderately at two-forty.

"There you are," gasped Frances, clutching Marcy's back and nearly bringing disaster to the tea run and a jam sandwich. "What do I do?"

"I'll get someone to take you round and introduce you to the President. Bring Miss Flayne with you."

Loveday and Frances looked at each other like two strange dogs, smiled and walked together, nervous for different reasons, to the side of the hall, where they sat self-consciously like new girls, until the bustling President, Mrs. Fanshawe, bore down on them with ruthless charm, thanked Frances for coming to their rescue, and vaguely welcomed Loveday.

"I madly said I'd give them a talk about the States," said Frances, as the chairs scraped and a small ferret of a woman approached the piano. Suddenly, to Loveday's surprise, they were all singing Blake's 'Jerusalem', the high notes quavered uncertainly round the rafters, but it was sung with a certain amount of enjoyment and purpose that Loveday found touching.

Mrs. Livers now came to the fore and read the minutes of the last meeting and there was a short argument about the desirability or not of a public convenience and the date of a whist drive. Then Frances found herself on her feet, a nerve twitching in her neck and her hand shaking.

"Speak up, my dear," said old Mrs. Grahame, sitting in the front row with her ear cupped. Frances raised her voice: "When I first went to America," she began . . . finding it not so difficult after all, and the applause at the end rang pleasantly in her ears as she made her way back to her seat at Loveday's side and was given a cup of strong tea by Marcy's hostesses who appeared with full trays from the back room. She thought as she looked at her audience how different they were from a similar gathering across the Atlantic. From where she sat she had a general impression of beiges and browns, unbecoming glasses, badly done

81

hair, depressing hats, yet even without the smarter heads and cared-for faces, there was that same earnest striving after something, they knew not what, to widen their lives.

"You were really very good," said Loveday.

"You sound rather surprised."

"Only because you seemed so frightened, but my father used to say American women talked about culture, horrible word, as if it were something concrete which lay about in lumps."

Frances looked again at Loveday and perceived that she did not fit in with the pattern round her. The blue tweed she wore had an air of well-cut newness and on her lapel was a silver ornament of curious beauty. Her bright eyes and smiling mouth gave a lightness to her expression, a feeling of gaiety which was contagious.

"Have you been to the States?" asked Frances.

"Not since the war, but before that in — when was it — in nineteen thirty-seven my father took me. He did a lecture tour. I didn't go with him, but I stayed in New

York and then with some friends of mine in Boston."

"You must meet my husband. He comes from Boston. Are you a friend of Marcy's?"

"Marcy?"

"Mrs. Lowesmore. That fat soul you were helping. I thought you must be a friend of hers."

"I'm nobody's friend," said Loveday. "I'm new, a visitor, Mrs. Livers brought me. I don't belong at all."

"Where do you live?"

"At Crafers, that square cottage up by the woods, beyond the Livers farm."

"Oh, I know, over the hill where Miss Cox used to live. Have you been there long?"

"Since February and I absolutely adore it, but of course it's all rather strange — " Loveday looked round at the chattering hubbub, feeling as if she might be on the mountains of the moon.

"You're not used to them, I guess. Nor am I. But I believe it's a wonderful thing. It saved Marcy's reason — the fat one, you know. She's really an aunt. My father was the eldest of a long family and

83

Marcy is only a bit older than we are and when my brother's wife died she came to look after Julian and the children. She has just thrown us all into panic by marrying Jack Lowesmore and going to live at Molesworth. I'm over for the summer and I hope by the time I go back I shall have organized something for them."

"Then the girl I met in the train is — ?"

"Ann. Did you meet her in the train? She's Julian's stepdaughter. She lives with her grandmother in London."

"Oh dear," sighed Loveday: "It's very complicated."

"Come back with me and meet them all."

"I'd love to. Would they mind?"

"Of course not. The entire neighbourhood use Friar's House as a sort of unofficial bus stop. It was Marcy's fault originally, but it's very disorganizing."

'That's twice she's used the word 'organize',' thought Loveday, but before she could consider the matter further she discovered that the cups had gone and the meeting had been swept into two teams. Frances rolled her eyes in mild derision on the other side of the room, and Loveday found herself involved in what looked like an adult version of 'Nuts in May' and while finding it all faintly ridiculous she had to admit afterwards, when her side had triumphantly defeated the others, that she was breathless and laughing and not wholly mocking.

Outside, Peter was standing by his red car and, as Loveday explained to Mrs. Livers that she was calling at Friar's House and would not be wanting a lift, he came forward and said; "Mr. Livers wanted the jeep so I said I'd fetch you."

He spoke to Mrs. Livers, but he looked at Loveday as he went on: "If you'll tell me what time you'll be ready I'll come down again."

He made this offer with an affronted air and Loveday protested that she could easily walk home.

"Nonsense," said Peter, stowing Mrs. Livers by his side. "It is going to be dark early and I'll bet you haven't brought a torch."

"No, I haven't," admitted Loveday,

"but that won't matter."

"I shall fetch you," said Peter patiently, "if you'll say the time."

"But I don't know the time," bleated Loveday, irritated by his persistence.

Without a word he put the car in gear and drove off, leaving her to realize that she had not even thanked him.

The study at Friar's House, which since the war years was the only room, other than the kitchen, where there was a fire, was long and rather dark. As Loveday advanced she saw Julian's head round the edge of a wing chair. He rose when he heard strange voices and Marcy switched on the light.

"I came home early because I felt like female companionship before the Parish Council meeting and found you all out and no fire," he said in an injured voice. The remains of a sordid tray of tea were at his side.

"Well, here we are, and I've brought Miss Flayne," said Frances making brisk introductions. "Isn't Ann back? She said she would fetch Roberta. Johnny is staying at school for tea because of his extra coaching. He's not coming until the six o'clock bus. Is Jack fetching you, Marcy?"

"I daresay," said Marcy easily, "or I might catch the bus. Frances always arranges everything as if she were a transport manager."

"Frances says she likes the peace and quiet of England and then gets us all in a turmoil. I'll get some sherry. I know it's early, but I'm sure Miss Flayne could do with some. What dissipation was it today?"

"Women's Institute, and Frances gave a talk," said Marcy.

Loveday sat in a shabby, not to say grubby, chair and was promptly joined by a cat which required to be stroked. She looked about her at the books, the pipes, the silhouettes on the walls, a puzzle on a tray in a corner and a general air of comfort without colour.

"And what did you think of it all?" asked Julian, pouring out sherry and handing a glass to Loveday.

"You told me I had to like everything in Overbridge," she answered.

"Did I? What a sweeping statement."

"It's lucky, but I do like everything,"

said Loveday happily. "Sometimes I admit I get a bit cross with Mr. Gorman."

"Ah, you've met him. We've all been cross with Mr. Gorman in our time, but he treats people with a sort of priority. If our boiler burst tonight . . . "

Everybody touched wood and crossed fingers and there was a general outcry that a listening Providence so tempted must be placated by all possible means.

"Or the chimney stack blows down, or a lorry hits the front door, he will leave everything and come to us."

"He'd leave my bathroom, of course."

"Of course," said Julian. "Rightly so. Our need would be greater than yours."

"One thing," remarked Loveday, "is that I shan't mind dying now I know there's such a pet of an undertaker in the place and such a heavenly view from the churchyard."

"I always feel he'd never get me properly below ground," said Marcy. "Someone's pipes would burst and he'd just leave me sticking out of my coffin."

"He'd have to, the size you are," said Julian. "Sherry? Before I have to go to the Council meeting."

Loveday said she wouldn't have any more and then found her glass full. She felt she should politely go, but the atmosphere of friendly bustle soothed and amused her and she thought, for the first time, of her chosen solitude at Crafers with slight distaste. Then as she drank the last of her sherry and rose the front door banged. There was laughter and high voices and suddenly the long narrow room was filled at one end with a small crowd who advanced half way and came no farther.

"It's Philippa Green and Miss Lavington. They have to catch the six bus and they only want to spend pennies."

Philippa laughed and Miss Lavington turned purple and backed into the hall again.

"I'm sorry," said Julian as his visitors were heard going upstairs. "Ann's generation are not very reticent."

"Good thing too," said Frances.

"Yes and No," said Loveday reflectively.

"Now you see why I voted for the Public Convenience," said Marcy.

"Hallo," said Ann briefly to Loveday.

"You're the one I met in the train."

Loveday smiled admission and stroked the leaping Tinker:

"She's grown," she said.

"Your car is waiting outside."

"I haven't got a car."

"Well, something is there at the door and as it annoys us to screaming point when people park there I asked what he was doing and he said he was waiting for you. A Jupiter it was, an old one — red."

"Then I really must go," said Loveday with regret, and she said good-bye and thank you hastily and collectively and was escorted by Julian to the front door.

"Quite pleasant," said Marcy, making up the fire as if she had never left its side.

"Her father was E. H. Flayne," said Frances.

"I never heard of him."

"He was an economist. We thought a lot of him in the States."

"Maybe, but it wouldn't make her any nicer."

"Don't you think it would be a good idea if we married her to Julian?"

Marcy dropped a log. "What an idea," she said.

"I know. It could be done though."

Marcy considered this.

"They'd still need someone for the rough, though," she said, "and Mrs. Herbage won't last much longer, poor old thing. I'd concentrate on that if I were you."

"A wife would be better," said Frances.

★ ★ ★

While conscious that she should be grateful to Peter for his kindness Loveday found herself suppressing irritation, for Peter, on being introduced to Julian, stood mulishly by his car door like a chauffeur until she was inside, and as they roared up the hill he did not speak.

"You shouldn't have bothered to come and fetch me," said Loveday at last.

"I didn't, I had to come down to the station with some chickens for Mrs. Livers."

"Oh," said Loveday rebuked, adding: "I could have walked up quite well."

"Not without a torch," said Peter severely. Then more gently: "I can lend you one. I've got two. You can't go around in the country at night without a torch."

"I'll buy myself a lanthorn, if you say so, you idiotic boy," said Loveday, laughing at last.

They were at her gate. She was tired, but she felt perhaps she should be polite and ask him in. He refused her gruffly, and Loveday, though relieved, let herself into her house, revived the fire, drew the curtains, switched on the light, turned on the radio and thought of her new book from the Times Book Club with pleasurable excitement. The rest of the evening was hers and she let its emptiness close round her.

6

The Birthday Party

"WE have been in England over two months," said Frances. "You ought to give a party for us."

It was a Saturday morning in May and Julian was eating a hasty lunch before going to Spedding to play golf.

"A party? But the place has been even fuller than usual ever since you arrived."

"But I mean a set party. What a bother! Don't you realize that I have a birthday next week? Give it on Saturday when Landon comes."

"Quite obviously," said Julian, rolling his napkin and tilting back his chair, "you have forgotten what an Overbridge party is like. Marcy says it's exactly the same as walking down Church Street on Saturday morning, except that no one carries a basket. You see all the same

93

people only they are in their best clothes. They say exactly the same things only louder and longer. If you ask them for cocktails, six to eight, they come at six and stay till eight, except four or five horrors, who linger until you have to give them supper. I am forced to go to parties, but I never give them."

"Then you should; think of Ann."

"You're not trying to tell me that Ann has a dull time."

"Well — no."

Truth compelled Frances to admit that Ann was seldom still long enough to consider whether she was dull or not, for Overbridge had a hockey club, a football club and a cricket club, and while Ann played none of these games, she was a kind of unofficial audience at the matches according to season. And in addition there was the Drama Society and a suggestion of Square Dancing. Between such engagements she drank coffee with her girl friends, gin with her boy friends, rode when she could borrow a horse, and was trying to make herself a dress for the Hospital Ball.

"Landon would be new, and I would

be fairly new and there's that Miss Flayne up at Crafers," said Frances.

"New blood indeed," said Julian, considering Miss Flayne up at Crafers, and his American brother-in-law. He was never sure if he liked Landon or not. As soon as he had decided that he really was a decent chap, Landon made some outrageous statement about Egypt or wore a tie with enormous gold beetles on it.

"All right," he said, giving in as he always did with swift submission after obstinate objections. "How much do you think they'll drink?"

Frances discovered that Crafers was not on the telephone, so she wrote a polite note to Loveday and posted it that very day. Mrs. Spracker brought it in on Monday, having met the postman. She also told Loveday that the Lenhams were giving a party and old Mrs. Herbage was going in an extra day to clean up, Loveday wasn't sure whether before or after the orgy. She was glad to be able to tell Mrs. Spracker that she was also invited, information that the lady hardly needed, so close was her finger on the pulse of Overbridge society.

"And I did wonder," went on Mrs. Spracker, "if them things in the trunk that you said could go to the Jumble would do for the Drammer. They've been asking for old-fashioned things, so I told Mrs. Fanshawe about them."

Loveday had found a trunk full of clothes in perfect preservation, musty and camphor ridden, and pathetically ridiculous. She had asked Mrs. Spracker what she should do with them and Mrs. Spracker was now telling her. In fact Mrs. Spracker assured Loveday that she would see to everything. Her brother-in-law, Norm Arbutt, the carrier, would take the whole trunk down, she didn't doubt, and Friar's House would be the best place 'because it was central'.

Loveday felt swift sympathy for Julian who said his home was like Paddington Station.

There was, as it happened, little need for any of this preliminary staff work, for no sooner had the Drama Society heard of Loveday's clothes than Ann was dispatched to inspect the offer.

It was raining and Loveday had her

feet up on Miss Cox's horsehair sofa, an object of such undeniable usefulness that Loveday had kept it, and covered it with honey-coloured corduroy. She had taken her shoes off and eaten the best part of a quarter of a pound of chocolates, and had then fallen into a light sleep, from which the sound of voices and bangs on her knocker disturbed her.

The unusualness of this proceeding brought her quickly to life. She kicked the chocolates under the sofa, and, failing to find her shoes, went sleepily to the door in her stockinged feet.

"It's only us," said Ann, "and this is Roberta. Are we being pests? We've come about the clothes."

Tinker, who was winding his long lead round Ann's feet added to the confusion, and when they had gone Loveday found she had finished off the chocolates.

"You'd better come up and see," said Loveday. "Mind your heads."

"Isn't it adorable, Roberta?"

Roberta frankly examined everything within reach and said it was 'cute'.

"We're doing a sort of pageant of Overbridge through the ages for the

97

Coronation," explained Ann.

Loveday began to unpack the trunk.

"I'm afraid they smell to high heaven of camphor. Let's have a look and see if any of the things will do. There's this blue dress, oh, and in that cupboard there's the most wonderful hat."

She stood on a chair and dropped a monumental hat adorned with roses on to Ann's head. It was ridiculous, but its size made it becoming and Ann looked up at Loveday, her full lips pouting, her nose tip-tilted, her urchin wisps submerged in the hat.

'What an adorable monkey she is,' thought Loveday. They both began to root in the trunk like dogs after a bone.

"This is heaven," said Ann. "Just look at this. You don't mean to say she had a waist that size? This is no good. It's falling to pieces."

They forgot Roberta, who put on a feather boa, picked up a Victorian paper-weight and went downstairs. After a while it dawned on Loveday that she was talking to someone.

"We'd better go down," she said, and, followed by Ann, still in the hat, she found Roberta at the kitchen door talking to Peter Coldfield. He carried a long parcel tied up in sacking, which looked like a thin and roughly shrouded corpse.

"I had to go to the station for Mrs. Livers and I saw this for you, so I brought it," he said. "They don't deliver up here until Thursday. They look like shrubs. It's very late for shrubs. Do you know how to plant them?"

"Of course," said Loveday shortly. She didn't, but surely you just dug a hole and put them in; that boy always inferred she could do nothing without his assistance.

"Where shall I put them?" he said meekly.

Loveday made herself say: "It really was kind of you. Just leave them in the shed. Won't you come in?"

He was over the mat in half a bound, encountering Ann as she came through the stair door. He gave the hat an astonished stare and Loveday introduced them.

"You'd better all stay to tea," said Loveday, picking up her book and putting the sofa back against the wall with a sigh. Amidst a barrage of chatter they demolished almost all her new bread and half an Australian Dundee cake which she hoarded for emergencies and the last of the chocolate biscuits. Loveday found to her horror that not only was she committed to seeing the pageant, but she had also, she knew not how, promised to help in the alteration of the clothes. It was not the peaceful afternoon she had planned, but she had enjoyed it extremely. The afternoon telescoped into evening with unusual speed.

When Ann and Roberta had gone Peter lingered and helped Loveday to light the fire.

"You should have taken them home," she said.

"My car is down at the farm," he excused himself easily.

"Don't you think Ann is enchantingly pretty?"

"No," he answered, surprised. He screwed up his eyes considering Ann. "Well, I suppose she is pretty," he said, "but so horribly young — "

"Poor old man, I suppose you must be every day of twenty-one."

"I'm twenty-four, nearly twenty-five. She only left school last year and she can't be more than eighteen. I like women to have more sense than they have at eighteen. Shall I fetch you some logs?"

"Please."

He brought the logs and she put them on the fire, staying on the hearth rug sitting on her heels. It was not yet dark and the fire lit the room companionably.

"Why did you come to live here?" he asked.

"Why? Oh, things happened, I wanted some peace. Why did you come?"

"Partly the same reason, I suppose."

She leant back on her heels and at the same time he leant forward from his chair to move a log. Whether by accident or design his hand touched her shoulder. For a moment neither of them moved. Then he said:

"Did you think you'd find peace?"

"One walks about with oneself," she answered; then as he did not take his hand away, she moved gently to her feet and snapped on the electric light.

He stood up as if he had been dismissed.

"It was kind of you to bring the shrubs."

"No, I had to go to the station."

All his former ungraciousness returned as he was gone.

* * *

One result of Loveday's visit to the Women's Institute was the fact that she found she recognized a number of people in the village who had, up till now, been just faces. She said 'Good morning' seven times between the post office and the butcher's and Mrs. Fanshawe, whom she recognized as the President, stopped and spoke to her and asked her if she could sing. On hearing that she could not she said it did not matter at all, only they had a Drama Group and a Choir, and no one could act or sing and Loveday simply must join. The Choir was every other Wednesday and the Drama on Tuesday evenings.

"I think I've lent some clothes to you.

Ann Forstal came up to see them," said Loveday.

"Ann — oh, that would be the Overbridge Players. Some of our people are in both — you could be in both if you are interested."

"I never thought of such a thing," said Loveday, suppressing a shudder. "I'd be no good at all at either."

She did manage to escape joining the Women's Institute Choir, but she never knew how it was that she became a member of the Drama Group. The President turned away exuding charm, enthusiasm and gratitude. She would have done well working for a press gang, thought Loveday, as she lunged into Miss Hollows's, who sold stationery, sweets and tobacco, and bought an engagement diary.

★ ★ ★

On the morning of the day fixed for the cocktail party at Friar's House, Ann woke in a bad temper. She was not alone in this. Frances, having passed over the stage of enthusiasm which drove her to

103

write the invitations and order potato crisps and cheese straws from Fortnum and Mason's, was now depressed by the paucity of glasses and the holes in the drawing-room carpet.

It was not, she told herself, that Julian couldn't afford a new carpet, he simply didn't care, and she didn't care either unless Landon was there. When Landon appeared she felt responsible for everything, from draughts to shabby carpets. She saw Overbridge, or thought she did, through American tinted spectacles.

In theory Julian did not work on Saturday mornings, but he generally found himself running over to see what was in the post and returning for a late lunch. This morning was no exception, but he was suffering from the effects of a sleepless night, for Johnny, who shared his bedroom when Landon was there, had coughed so heartrendingly in the night, though without complaint, that Julian had lain awake long after Johnny had fallen into a wheezing sleep. All the unpleasant thoughts that night unfolds took distorted shape in his brain. The house seemed overfull and Frances, though efficient, was less comfortable than Marcy, and Heaven knew she was maddening enough. In spite of the fullness of the house, a fact which irked him in itself, he had at four in the morning a feeling of being alone and cut off and misunderstood.

He wondered if he would be more contented if a woman were in the bed where Johnny lay uneasily, or even at closer quarters, someone gentle and loving, and of course beautiful; someone who would make him laugh and hold him close and give him the warmth and comfort of her body; a paragon whom he was as unlikely to meet in Overbridge as elsewhere.

Pursued by this tantalizing vision he decided to go downstairs and make some tea as dawn began to lighten the shadows, and in the kitchen, warming herself by the boiler, he found Ann.

"Good Heavens, child, what are you doing?"

"Getting some tea; I couldn't sleep."

"At your age, well, fish out another cup for your step-father and let me get near some warmth."

He pulled his old camel-hair dressing-gown more closely round him and his sandy hair stuck up at the back so that he looked a little like Johnny.

"I had a row with Frances about this perishing party," said Ann, pouring out the tea.

"Did you? So did I," answered her father. "At least, not a row exactly."

"Well, I did, a proper brawl. It was while you were at that meeting. I said I didn't want to be there; you've only asked a whole lot of greybeards and hags."

"We haven't."

"But you have, darling," persisted Ann; "There isn't a soul under forty, I swear."

"Oh well, perhaps you're right there, but it's for Frances, you know," said Julian, smiling and wondering at what stage in life forty ceased to be regarded as the onset of senility.

"I'm sure it's going to be ghastly, so I'm going to London on the eight o'clock train and I shall stay the night with Granny. Don't look so scandalized."

"I'm not scandalized, but I think it's damnation rude."

He gulped the sweet tea and felt suddenly sleepy. He didn't want to argue with Ann, he wanted to go back to bed. He found he was about to say, 'When I was your age . . . ' and checked himself.

"Don't you even want to know what I'm going to do there?" asked Ann, disconcerted by his silence.

"Of course I do, but if you don't tell me how can I know? You needn't think I'm going to ask."

"As a matter of fact," said Ann, peering into the boiler to make sure it was still going. "I'd quite like you to ask. No one seems a bit interested in me."

"My dear child, what do you want, in Heaven's name? I thought parents, even step-ones, had to leave the young alone. And I don't bring you up after all. That's your grandmother's job. You are very hard to understand."

"I don't want to be understood. Can't you see that? I want to be told what to do."

Her voice suddenly became loud and emphatic.

"Sh — " whispered her father.

She took no notice.

"I can't decide everything — all by myself."

Julian's sleepiness vanished. He saw his step-daughter clearly as a person outside the circle of his family.

"What do you want decided for you?" he asked.

"Masses of things, whether it's any good going on with Henry."

Up went Julian's eyebrows.

"You see," Ann went on, "you don't know even who he is, and I've been in love with him for nearly three months."

"Well, tell me about him."

"He's a pilot on Antipodean Airways and he has black hair and blue eyes and a little moustache like Cesar Romero's."

Julian subdued a shudder.

"And I think he's mad about me too, in patches, when I'm there," continued Ann. "I thought he was going to be away for six months and then I heard he was back for a week, so I thought I'd dash off and — "

"Is that very sensible?"

"No, it's idiotic, I know, but I just can't help myself.

"You don't — "

"Sleep with him?" said Ann frankly. "No. He wants to, of course, but somehow I didn't really care about the idea when it came to it; men are awfully vain, aren't they, Daddy? They think you're cold or early Victorian, or a prude, but never that they aren't always awfully alluring."

Julian poured out some more tea. He heard the alarm clock ring unchecked in his room above. He was appalled at his step-daughter's revelations while admiring her clear vision.

"What do want me to do?" she said.

He had, he supposed, to be wise and broadminded at all costs, Marcy said so — Frances said so — all the articles in the Sunday papers said so, but what he replied was: "Good Lord, Ann, drop the man and stamp on his face."

"Darling, you don't do that any more."

"Great pity," said Julian. "I feel like horse-whipping him, if I had a horse-whip," he added. "Don't you know a scoundrel when you see one? I'm surprised that you're such a fool, and what's more, my child, I'm damned if I'll let you go to London at all. You stay here and help with this confounded party or else — "

"All right," said Ann, with a meekness that surprised him.

All this Julian thought over as he sat at his desk in Hinwood and played with a paper-knife. His office had the forsaken look of all offices on Saturday since the inauguration of the five-day week. It was without the peace of Sunday, for outside the Saturday traffic and the scurrying women with baskets denied this, but the empty chairs around him, ghostly before the hooded typewriters, and the few torn envelopes on his own desk depressed him. The sun shone obliquely through the dusty window. It was too late to play golf and he wondered like a small boy what he should do. It was no use going home, for furniture was being moved with abandon from A to B and back again. Landon was to arrive at one-fourteen and must be met and it was now just after eleven. Julian seldom drank before six o'clock, but today he looked across the Market Place at the Three Tuns with its grey uninviting windows and saw in his mind's eye the warm bar beyond. He locked the door behind him and strode into the street, nearly knocking down a small woman in grey. He raised his hat and apologized.

"Good morning, Mr. Lenham," smiled the apparent stranger. "If you knock me down I shan't be able to come to your party."

Unless Julian had some special reason for remembering a woman, her extreme beauty or ugliness, or perhaps indeed, her bad manners, he seldom recognized anyone until he knew her well. Horror-struck, he looked at Loveday, wondering where it was that he had encountered those amused eyes before.

"You don't remember me, and why should you? My name is Flayne — " She began to pass on towards the square.

Recognition dawned in his eyes, and in his haste to make amends he detained her politely.

"Of course I know you. Are you shopping? Can I give you a lift home?"

"That's very kind, but I'm afraid not. I have to wait while my little wireless is being finished, and I was just going to kill time having coffee."

"May I come with you? I'm killing time too. I daren't go home or I'd be given some work. How long will the job take?"

"About three quarters of an hour, Davis said. I only come in once a week and I can't bear to be without it any longer."

"Do you get lonely up there?"

"Most people ask that and the answer is 'No', but I hate being without a radio. People are very kind. I'm quite amazed at it after London. I had a bad cold last week and Mrs. Livers came and brought me meals, and young Colefield kept my fire going, and Mrs. Spracker did my shopping. It was so refreshing I felt like taking to my bed entirely and just radiating sweetness and light."

★ ★ ★

Hinwood had two coffee-houses. One was large, on three floors, furnished cheerfully in red leather and chromium and with bright iced cakes and buns oozing bogus cream. The other was small, low-beamed and the cakes were home-made. Julian

112

preferred the latter, but as the larger one was on the corner of the Market Square he led the way into it and up the stairs. It was full but they found a table at last, and Loveday put her basket out of the way of his feet and inquired politely after his family.

It would have been pleasant, reflected Julian, to have told this small creature about Ann, about Johnny, about Marcy, about Frances, even about Judy, but he simply said: "They're fine, thank you," adding, "except Johnny. He has asthma, you know, devilish thing. I don't know whether to send him away to school or not."

"I should," said Loveday's quiet voice.

"Would you? Would it be worth trying?"

"Don't you think perhaps asthmatic children feel the anxiety in you about themselves and the tension causes the asthma?"

"I wonder. I hadn't thought of it like that. Of course one tries not to show one's anxiety. Do you know anything about it from personal experience?"

"Only from watching," answered

Loveday. "I've had to do a lot of looking on in my life. I have a godchild with asthma. The odd thing is he never has an attack when he stays with me."

"That may be the place."

"Possibly."

He liked talking to this woman. She argued quietly, as if she saw your point of view and was loth to convince you. He leaned his head on his hands and looked across the table at her.

Loveday, under his scrutiny, wished that this bright May day was not swept by an east wind, for she was cold, and cold she knew had a deadening effect on all except the most youthful attractions. But she talked with him cheerfully about Overbridge's preparations for the Coronation, a film which neither of them had seen and the poorness of the bus service, and when they parted they both found that the party in the evening, to which neither of them had been looking forward with any pleasure, had turned into an occasion when they would meet again.

★ ★ ★

Peter had said so many times: 'Whenever you want to go to the village let me know and I'll take you in the car.' But as a rule Loveday enjoyed the walk, particularly when it was dry enough to go through the copse and the vicarage fields to emerge at the insanitary Tudor backs of the Georgian-fronted street.

In the past weeks Peter had been so helpful, mending a fuse, getting her coal and fetching and carrying while she had a bad cold that she was not ready to ask him to do more. She wished, not for the first time, that she had a son. If she had married early by now she ought to have been leaning on the arm of a stalwart son. 'More likely,' she thought, giving herself a mental shake, 'a spotty weed who argued with me.' Her own friends' struggles with their adolescent children had been something with which she used to assuage her occasional pangs of childlessness and spinsterhood.

Tonight, however, she thought she did not care to arrive at Julian's with her party face blown off by the wind and Peter on Saturdays always went down to the Duke's Head to play darts. She put on her gum-boots and walked across the field to his caravan.

He opened the door, eating an apple, his finger in a book, and took off a record of the Brandenburg Concerto which was making the caravan shake with sound.

"Are you going to the village tonight?" she asked.

"No, why? Do you want me to?"

"Not if you aren't going down to the village."

"Oh, but I could — easily."

"No, I shall get a taxi."

"That only means trekking to the main road to telephone. Tell me what you want and I'll do it for you."

"You're very good natured."

"So are you." He grinned.

"I'll never get over refusing you that bucket of water," sighed Loveday, sitting at the table flap and drinking the tea which he now gave her in a steaming mug.

"Well, this is just in the nature of coals of fire. Tell me what you want fetching."

"Nothing, I just want to be taken down to the Lenham's, about half-past six. He's going to bring me back."

"Who?"

"Mr. Lenham."

"Oh."

He was such a transparent child, thought Loveday. By the back of his neck, the set of his ear, and the curve to the corner of his mouth as he bent over the gramophone, Loveday knew he was hurt. She thought it was because he hadn't been asked to the party, since he now knew Ann.

"It's his sister's birthday, rather older people are asked, I gather. Mr. Lenham told me that Ann was going to have another one later on for her contemporaries. I expect you'll be asked to that."

"But you won't."

"No, of course not."

"Oh."

He could make 'Oh' sound many things. Loveday drank the tea and was silent.

"I'll honk about half-past six," he said.

"You really are a kind boy."

"Wish you wouldn't call me a boy. I'm twenty-four."

"So you keep telling me. It's great age. Well, I must go."

"Oh don't, you never come to see me. Don't rush off."

"I must, it will take me hours to get fit for this party. Even my frock will have to be aired and as for my hands — " She spread them out in disgust, gardening and housework had wreaked their usual havoc.

He caught one of her hands, looked at it calmly and released it, saying. "Why bother?"

★ ★ ★

As she rubbed cream into her hands, soaked in the bath, painted her nails, pressed her claret-coloured dress and searched for her ruby and pearl earrings, Loveday wondered whether any party could possibly be worth the effort — even the first one for three months. She cast her mind back to her life of the year before, the sudden bouts of hospitality, the casual visitors, the parties hard on each other's heels, as she went to the cupboard for her fur coat. It was an

118

old one of her mother's, remade, and the summer ermine was softly flattering. She put perfume behind her ears and slipped her feet into high-heeled shoes, instantly feeling inches taller and completely ready for any party.

Peter banged on the knocker and walked in, calling her name. Since she had had the cold he did not wait for the door to be opened to him and Loveday could not make up her mind whether this pleased her or not.

"I'm coming," she called, switched off her bedroom light, and ran quickly down the stairs. She felt gay, young, as if it were twenty years ago and she was going to a dance, only then she had always wondered if she would have a good time. Now she did not care.

He stood and looked at her. "You look smashing," he said. The adjective was one which revolted Loveday, but she took it in the spirit in which it was meant, as she walked with him to the car, stepping carefully to keep her shoes clean.

"What a shame you aren't coming."

"Isn't it? Especially in these clothes?"

He looked at his dirty flannels and tartan shirt.

★ ★ ★

The door was opened by Roberta and Johnny and from somewhere at the back of the house came a high-pitched roar. It was Julian's forty-three guests trying to make their witticisms heard.

Roberta's red ribbons drew back her hair so that they seemed to be pulling her eyebrows aslant. With quite frightening poise she took Loveday into the little morning room to shed her coat and Johnny opened the door and said loudly: "Miss Flayne," giggled, and withdrew. No one had even heard him and Loveday stood for a moment, not shy, because her life had cured her of shyness, but merely regretting the foolishness of looking forward to a form of entertainment which experience had shown her was often tiresome. The mood lasted until the drink which Ann gave her had warmed her inward vision and Julian found her talking to Landon.

Landon felt as strange as Loveday. To

his mind these cocktails were not strong enough or cold enough and the women were unspeakably drab. He noticed Loveday because she was, though not better dressed, better groomed than the others, and having brought her a drink, he said in his flat Bostonian accent, which gave a foreign fillip to the most inane remark:

"My wife tells me you were in the States with your father. My mother went to one of his lectures at the Garden Club in Boston. I remember her telling us about it. We argued for days."

"Yes, Father nearly got torn apart sometimes. But he was a gentle old thing really."

He was dead and already she had forgotten his tyranny. She remembered only his chiselled brain and popularity grudgingly gained by sheer integrity of mind.

Landon knew that she would ask him if he liked England. This unanswerable question had been fired at him by everyone to whom he had spoken so far. It was impossible to answer it truthfully for at the slightest hint of criticism the spirit of Sir Francis Drake and the Duke of Wellington blazed fiercely from all British hearts and dulled their reason. If, on the other hand, they told him that they knew he hated the damp and the warm beer and the bad coffee, some of the things he did indeed hate, he found himself denying this with heat.

Politics he had found also a source of acrimony and business methods another and his conversation came strangely to dwell on two subjects which he never discussed at home and on which he was ill-informed, films and food. The British, he discovered, since the hardships of war, could talk for hours on food, the thought of steaks and chicken *Maryland* and frosted layer cakes brought the same expression to their eyes that a woman brings to an Italian's — they drooled.

Loveday and Landon were clearly the only people in the room who did not know everybody else. Loveday had been the last to appear, for Overbridge, whose parties were seldom, arrived at the time stated, six-thirty, and would not go until eight o'clock at least, as Julian had forseen. Introductions were few, though

122

Marcy and Julian made some attempt to the few whom she did not know. The cocktails, which were deficient in ice, had been mixed in washing jugs in the kitchen with much laughter earlier in the day, and a few people who were entrusted with smaller glass jugs mingled with the throng refilling glasses. Johnny, who would normally have been in bed, had been allowed to stay up as it had never occured to Roberta to do anything else, and the two were inseparable; they carried plates of cocktail snacks which they shamelessly plundered as they wound their way under people's elbows.

It grew hotter, the talk became louder, the laughter shriller. Loveday thought longingly of the radio programme she was missing. She had recognized various faces, which she had encountered shopping or on the bus, a few from the Women's Institute, the Vicar, and a large man, jovial as a monk, who, she thought, was the doctor. Her greatest success was with Johnny. As his father had promised to take her home she was perforce one of the last to leave. She found a chair and lost herself in it while Johnny and Roberta perched on the arms.

When Julian at last had time to speak to her the party had thinned to a dozen. Loveday and the children were deep in a talk on stamp collecting.

"She says she's got some stamps I can have."

"Not 'she',' 'Miss Flayne'." corrected Julian.

"Yes, Miss Flayne. She says she's got a Roumanian one I can have and they cost three and six."

"Don't give him anything valuable," said Julian.

"But they aren't any use if they're not valuable, are they, Johnny," smiled Loveday.

"Of course not."

"They were my father's and my nephew isn't interested. Are you wanting me to go?"

"Not wanting you to. I simply haven't seen you. Worst of these blasted parties. But I've got to take the Trants back to Upper Spedding and I could drop you on the way."

"I'll get my coat."

Someone opened a window. A chill blew through the room. Bereft of the guests it was bare, with the furniture moved out of the way into unfamiliar corners. Frances looked tired and the children were skirmishing over the last olive. Landon walked half-heartedly round with a jug.

Loveday and the Trants, now introduced for the first time, appeared in their coats, apologizing for causing trouble by not owning cars. Two people, whom Loveday did not know, lingered, obviously intending to stay for supper. 'Good-byes' were said, and Marcy began to empty the ashtrays. The party was over.

★ ★ ★

At her gate, as she heard Julian's car move on with the Trants, Loveday realized she had no torch. It was part of her equipment which she was forever forgetting. She felt the wet bushes brushing her skirt and her nylons, by a soundless sensation, as light as a kiss, gave notice that they had laddered.

She found the key, which was so large that she had given up carrying it in her bag and hid it recklessly under a stone. In her sitting-room the fire was nearly out, but when she blew with Miss Cox's bellows a flame curled round the coals and cheered the air. In a few moments loud laughter from the radio brought her vicarious companions and she drew the curtains. The party which she had not really enjoyed had made her restless. It was too early for bed, too late to start something. Glorious and rather chilly in her best dress she sat down and thought with distaste of mending stockings.

* * *

At Friar's House they were tearing the party to pieces, sitting comfortably round the fire. Marcy's husband and the doctor and his wife, who had lingered to a bacon and egg supper and the last of the cocktails, were old enough friends to appreciate the pastime.

"Mrs. Hopkins's hat looked exactly

like a hot-water bottle cover," said Faith Hove.

"It was a hot-water cover," laughed Marcy.

Julian went upstairs for the third time with threatening words for Johnny and Roberta, who were too excited to go to sleep.

"I thought that Flayne woman looked surprisingly pretty," said Landon.

"Why surprisingly, darling," objected Frances. "Don't think all the looks are in the States."

"Well, you know," drawled Landon, "you do look sometimes as if you'd all got into something loose."

Marcy laughed good-naturedly. "And me with my best corsets killing me."

Her fat ankles bulged above her shoes which she kicked off.

Julian came back and said he wondered how she could live all alone up at Crafers. Frances looked at Marcy and winked. Her imagination was already marrying Julian to Loveday in a Register Office, or perhaps quite quietly at the Parish Church. If they bestirred themselves it could be fixed before she left for the

States. Roberta could be a bridesmaid. Her imagination happily bridged time and space.

The Hoves said they must go. Julian yawned and thought of the peace of his bed and whether the body in Chapter Three of his new thriller had been killed by the charwoman or the body's sister. Fifty more pages of delicious horror awaited him.

Then the telephone rang.

An American voice asked for Landon and the telephone being in a public corner everyone listened with one ear, while making elaborate pretence of doing nothing of the kind.

Finally Landon put his hand cautiously over the mouthpiece and said to Frances: "It's K.K. He came down to Exton to see his brother in the Air Force and his car has broken down about five miles along the main road and he thought of us — "

"Is he sober?" asked Frances swiftly.

"Why, yes, I suppose so. He sounded O.K. to me."

The quick easy hospitality of her adopted country made Frances say to

128

Julian: "Could we fix him in somewhere? Have you got a cot we could put up in the play-room?"

"We put anything up to four-year-olds in cots," said Marcy. "Who is he, anyway."

'Any moment,' thought Landon, looking at their faces, 'They'll up with the drawbridge and out with the boiling oil.'

Frances explained quickly. "He's Kevin Kelly — works at the Embassy — Landon was at College with him."

A swift vision composed of a mixture of nylons, tins of steak and manly charm floated past Ann's eyes.

"I'll sleep on the sofa down here," she said, "and he can have my room."

Julian realized suddenly that he was master of the house, as Landon looked at him questioningly, and said: "He can have my room. I'll sleep on the sofa," thinking with distaste amounting to horror of more talk — more people.

Landon spoke quickly to the telephone, giving instructions about taxis and how to find the house and Marcy began to gather up the glasses and wash up as if she had never left the kitchen.

"I say," said her husband, speaking for the first time in half an hour, "aren't we going home?"

"When I've washed up," said Marcy.

Frances and Ann protested. Landon was still talking to the troublesome K.K. "You turn left at the cross-roads and through the village. It's by the church."

Julian shut both the doors and stood in an oasis of stillness in the hall. The dogs' lead dangling from a hook reminded him that they must be taken for their evening run. Landon came out of the sitting-room in apologetic mood.

"I say, I'm more than sorry. It was only by chance that he knew I was here, but we were telling him about you all at lunch last week."

Julian protested with some attempt at conviction that it was perfectly all right. As he attempted to fix the lead he felt dull with weariness.

★ ★ ★

When he returned from walking the dogs across the churchyard every window of

Friar's House blazed with light. In the hall stood an expensive-looking suitcase and in his study, amidst a babble of laughter and talk, Frances was dispensing what Julian suspected was the last bottle of gin.

K.K., who was the centre of the group, greeted him with polite words of gratitude.

'If only I could go to bed,' thought Julian desperately.

Marcy and Jack had gone, but the room seemed as full as ever and had still the faintly disreputable air of all rooms at midnight after a party.

K.K. and Landon, though of different ages and colouring and build had, by a similarity in tailoring and haircut, a brotherly air. Ann, receiving attention at last, was perched on the arm of a chair shaking her short hair like a poodle after a swim. Frances's voice was two tones higher, and Roberta suddenly appeared from nowhere in a nightgown and pensively ate potato crisps. Johnny, not to be outdone, also appeared and, as Julian shooed them both back and saw them skip protesting up the stairs, he realized that Johnny had not had an attack of asthma since — since Frances came home from America.

'If I'm to keep awake,' he thought, 'I'll have to have another drink.'

He saw with dismay that the bottle was nearly empty and then comforted himself with the thought that when it was they would all go to bed. The blissful anticipation of his sheets and soft pillow and a shut door lured him to his bed like a mistress, until he remembered that he had to sleep on the sofa. He looked at the clock. It was a quarter to one.

* * *

He was surprised to find that he slept reasonably well, waking at seven as usual with a crick in his back where the sofa did not fit him. As he lay looking at the disordered room, the drooping flowers, the bedclothes adding the last squalid touch, he missed Marcy acutely. Marcy, he thought, would have brought him a cup of tea.

Such amenities meant nothing to Frances after years in America, while

Ann would sleep, unless she was worried, while the house fell to pieces around her. And Ann, he was relieved to think, had gone to bed gay and excited, for K.K., with the disarming directness of his kind, had already made plans for going over Witstone Castle with her and taking her out to lunch.

K.K., thought Julian, was pleasant enough, but he wished Ann would soon reach the stage where she discriminated. A corner of his mind still worried about Ann as he hauled himself at last from the sofa and slopped in his slippers across to the kitchen to make some tea.

As the kettle boiled the room filled with Marcy's fat ghost.

He found himself envying Jack Lowesmore.

7

God Save The Queen!

EARLIER in the year there had been a public meeting in Overbridge to decide on its part in the Coronation celebrations and Mrs. Livers had made it plain that it was Loveday's duty to go. Duty came to have a new meaning in Overbridge and, in the spring, when the Coronation seemed inevitably very far off, on a day of unbelievable sunshine, it seemed a little untimely to Loveday to be worrying about flags and decorated bicycles, and where to borrow an urn. But she obediently went to the meeting and sat with the Livers in the front row where she was noticed by the Vicar, who was Chairman, and so found herself committed to various time-taking activities, such as collecting money for the Old Folks' Tea and washing up on 'The Day'. Julian was the Treasurer and dispensed and collected small sums with miser-like exactitude.

Being such a small cog in the wheel she was only half aware of the general pre-Coronation bustle, of Mrs. Fanshawe's taking offence, of old Mrs. Tressle's awkwardness, of how Miss Fotherton never came to the meetings and then expected to be first in everything. She was touched by the amount of work done by everyone and full of admiration for the way the Vicar ignored people's feelings and got on with the job. By the eve of the Coronation she had every sympathy with the Duke of Norfolk.

And then it rained and the flags which had fluttered so bravely across the street in the hot days of Whitsuntide hung with obstinate gaiety, wet, clinging. The folk dancing was cancelled, the decorated bicycles were drenched and the organizers of the sports rushed about with blue faces while children slipped and slithered through the races on the muddy recreation ground and had their photographs taken for the local paper.

Loveday had felt she wanted to spend the morning alone. Peter was in London and intended to stand all night on the corner of St. James's Street and Loveday had been asked to share the Livers' television, but she felt she had to listen quietly on her own radio and be there in her mind. Afterwards, she regretted this, but she sat peacefully doing her mending and listening so intently that she was transported to the Abbey, moved to tears by the solemn beauty of the young Queen's dedication to her people.

At three o'clock she put on her mackintosh and started out, not without a feeling of distaste, for the Old Folks' Tea.

There had been a certain amount of coyness by the elderly as to what constituted Old Folks and a number of sprightly sixty-year-olds, who looked ten years younger, were quite naturally loth to take old folks' status, so that the party consisted of a collection of what looked like the oldest inhabitants of any village, and a certain number of spongers after a 'meat tea'.

The three women who were in charge of the washing-up greeted Loveday, for they were all members of the Women's Institute, and if they did not know her personally they knew who she was and were prepared to be friendly. They threw detergents into the water in a lavish and masterful way, told Loveday where the towels were, and agreed that the Queen had looked lovely. The peculiar smell of damp, escaping gas and mice, which was part of the back room atmosphere of the Memorial Hall had by now, for Loveday, a home-like feeling. Here she had first met the members of the Women's Institute, here the Drama Society meetings were held, because it was cheaper than taking the larger hall. She knew that the tap dripped, how to manage the shilling-in-the-slot meter and where the lavatories were.

When Marcy arrived with a car-load of jellies and trifles she was greeted warmly and Loveday was instructed by Mrs. Fanshawe, who automatically took the role of forewoman in most village activities, to help her move them in. Everything was done with the maximum amount of energy and difficulty. No one thought of saving anybody steps or work because there was always a surplus of labour, volunteers such as

Miss Kennington and old Mrs. Dacre, always willing, so long as they never had to take any responsibility.

Backwards and forwards walked Loveday and Miss Kennington, down the long concrete path between the Memorial Hall and the doctor's surgery, until all the jellies and trifles, with only minor casualties, were laid out upon trestle tables.

When it was discovered that the Youth Club, who had last used the urn, had put it away damp and it now smelt musty there was a certain amount of hard feeling. Mrs. Fanshawe said it was absolutely disgraceful, rolling her 'r's' and her eyes in a manner to shrivel her hearers, but Marcy, by merely chuckling over all her chins and lumbering up and down the two steps into the kitchen sideways, like an enormous crab, managed to restore them all to good humour.

There were two schools of thought about the food. Mrs. Fanshawe thought there was too much. Marcy thought there was not enough and Loveday never had time to discover who was right, for as soon as the guests arrived she was kept busy under Mrs. Fanshawe's orders, serving soft drinks and later tea and coffee, and at the end she looked round and saw nothing but a pile of crusts off the sandwiches.

Above the clatter of the washing up they heard the strains of 'God Save the Queen' and stood loyally to attention, cloth in hand. Loveday's feet hurt and her head was beginning to ache. She stared across the back room at a large engraving of Queen Victoria and her children, and thought with a wave of pity of the weight of a crown.

With bursts of laughter and farewells the guests went out into the June rain. The chaos of washing-up, with a multitude of helpers began to lessen, to diminish, to end, until the back room was restored to order, and the china was locked up with great ceremony and two padlocks by Mrs. Fanshawe, and the keys hidden in a place known to all, on the top of the gas-meter. Miss Kennington said there were thirteen teaspoons short and Mrs. Baines asked what she should do with a broken cup. Marcy was wiping milk off the gas stove so as not to offend the caretaker. Loveday was concealing her charms in a mackintosh and head-scarf, and regretting that she had not ordered a taxi when she was aware of Julian standing by the door.

"I say, Marcy, Jack is at Friar's House recovering and I said I'd bring you along. What about you, Miss Flayne? Can I run you up the hill?"

Marcy forgot she was no longer mistress of Friar's House and offered its hospitality as if it were her own.

"Julian, Miss Flayne and I are corpses, I tell you, corpses. We must have some tea."

"But I've been eating and drinking all the evening," protested Loveday. "I had crusts off the sandwiches and two jellies that were knocked over and countless cups of coffee because we miscalculated and there was heaps over."

"But you'd like to come in and recover, wouldn't you?" said Julian. "If the Queen feels anything like the way I do after those terrible sports she's in no shape to come out on to the balcony."

Everyone agreed that the Queen was

wonderful and the Duke of Edinburgh and the children and the Queen Mother and Princess Margaret. They went all through the Royal Family talking about them as if they were rather special relations, regaling tit-bits from the Sunday papers, and worrying if they had seen any of them looking sad and tired or unhappy. It was a state of mind and emotion which was hard to explain, a sort of loving exaltation.

Everyone, except Ted Grosshorn, the local Communist, was melted with loyalty. They loved the Queen and the Royal Family, they loved each other. The acrimony which was to arise over whether a seat or a swing for the children should be bought out of the surplus money, and the disclosure of the mug-less state of the children in Station Road, due to the harassment of the schoolmistress, who had to arrange a pageant of Overbridge through the Ages by her scholars, all of whom were under eleven, lay in the mists of the future.

In Overbridge on this Coronation night of Queen Elizabeth the Second all was peace and joy. It had stopped raining and the streets shone in the gay lights streaming out of the three public houses. The flags whipped against the walls, the gold lion and the unicorn on the butcher's was peeling a little and poor Miss Kennington's paper decorations had disintegrated, leaving red, white and blue streaks on her door, but everything was enlivened by shooting rockets and warmed by the light of a great fire.

"The bonfire," cried Loveday. "Why, we've forgotten the bonfire. It's in Livers' field. We should get a lovely view from my cottage. You must all come up and see it."

So they all drove up to Crafers. Not only Julian and Johnny and Marcy and her husband, but everyone within earshot considered themselves included, and when the guests eventually turned out of the cars there were many more than Loveday intended, and two girls whom she could not place at all, though she vaguely remembered seeing them in one of the shops.

Loveday's sitting-room was already bright with the light of the fire in Livers' field, so that some of them could have a grand-stand view in comfort. But there was not room for more than a few and most of the guests wandered out through the back door and perched on the low wall like a row of cats.

Loveday brought out an immense enamel tea-pot which had belonged to Miss Cox and dispensed tea all round. She ran out of milk, but Miss Kennington remembered that she had two pints in her basket which were over from the Social and she rushed out and brought them in from Mrs. Fanshawe's car. Everyone gave a hand. Every cup in the house came into use, including an old Coalport one off the sitting-room mantelpiece and two without handles which Loveday had not thrown away.

Afterwards she realized that she had hardly had time to see the bonfire, until Julian told her to come and look at Upper Spedding Church. It had been flood-lit and away on the skyline there it hung, suspended in a glow which took away its sturdy Norman depth and displayed it like some unreal painted image on a dark blue background.

Mrs. Fanshawe was most indignant that Overbridge had not had the idea first and the feeling of the meeting was that to light Upper Spedding Church bordered almost on sharp practice.

"But Overbridge Church is so enclosed hardly anyone but those cottages at the corner would see it," objected Loveday.

Everyone looked at Loveday as if she had made some traitorous suggestion. She laughed at their shocked faces: "You must admit," she went on, "that Upper Spedding has the advantage of the perfect position. I should like to see it from the valley the other side."

The fire was almost out now, the fireworks were used up, the black imps who had been dancing and shrieking round it, and the dervishes who had been stoking it came back to reality and became a pack of school children and the local scouts, who were in charge of the display under the care of the schoolmaster. They stamped out the last embers, helped in efficiency by the gusts of rain which had just started again. As the laughter and voices died away, one tall solitary scout hovered about like a lean vulture picking up the litter, whirling in the cold wind. The row of people on the wall shivered, and began to say 'Good-bye.'

"Someone," pleaded Loveday, "someone please fetch that scout and give him some tea. I am so thankful to see him clearing up."

Miss Kennington said it was Bob Finch, who when fetched turned out to be the third face in the choir on the right going in. He drank the last of the tea without saying a word and was taken home by Julian.

When they had all gone, Loveday began to wash up the cups. Nothing so pleasant, so companionable, so gay had happened to her before. She tried to imagine such a party fitting into her London life and could not.

Miss Kennington had that very evening announced that she had only been to London once and it was 'that noisy she was glad to get home' and she thought it possible that Bob Finch had never been there at all, for one of the drawbacks or advantages of Overbridge, it depends how you look at it, is that it is impossible to travel to London and back in the day and spend any time there. This Coronation year, however, there were to be special excursions from Hinwood Junction, starting at 5.30 a.m., and all sorts of expeditions 'to see the lights' were being planned by the various village organizations.

Loveday dried the cups and put them away. It was midnight. The rain was beating against her sturdy cottage. All along the hills the fires were out. The radio told her that the young Queen and her husband had just appeared on the balcony at Buckingham Palace.

She lay down in Miss Cox's high bed. It was a curious wooden one, obviously made without pretensions by some country carpenter, with the head and foot equal in height, like a French peasant's bed, or a child's cot.

It was comfortable and Loveday stretched thankfully, thinking of the young Queen.

'I hope she is not too tired,' murmured Loveday drowsily to herself. 'I hope they keep her safe — and happy.'

8

Coronation Excursions

THE next day some of the travellers returned with varying descriptions of the Great Day. Landon's firm had lavishly taken a whole floor in Piccadilly and Frances and Roberta, who had been invited, came home still carried away by the excitement and the colour. Ann had stayed the night with her grandmother in Buckingham Gate, had walked on to the route at the last moment, and had most annoyingly seen everything, and had been back at the flat in time for the television. Peter had camped for thirty-six hours in the Mall, spent another night in the station, soaked to the skin, and had gone straight to bed to recover, but Johnny was the most excited of all. He had won the decorated bicycle race at the Overbridge Children's Sports and had had his photograph in the *Hinwood Chronicle*. This had, in some measure, compensated him for not going to London with Roberta. Julian had decided it would have been too exciting for him and he, being used to his pleasures taking second place to his asthma, after a threat of tears, took the decision with unchildlike philosophy. When Julian eventually tucked Johnny up after midnight, his eyes blue-ringed and his cheeks hot with the excitement of the festivities at Overbridge, including a thorough drenching, he wondered if London could have been more exhausting.

There was a certain feeling of hangover about the next two days. The weather was cold. Everyone who was not clearing up the remains of the Coronation, returning crockery, making up accounts or repairing damage, remained in a state of suspended animation until the Coronation film came to the nearest cinema at Hinwood. People like the Misses Hinks, who had not set foot in a cinema since the days of the silent films, when they had been shocked by the Queen of Sheba, to ardent fans like Mrs. Spracker, saw the performance through three times, queued at the box office. As the programme included an

148

American film of astonishing dullness and vulgarity this might be considered a touching sign of loyalty.

Loveday decided that she would combine a shopping expedition to Hinwood with lunch and a visit to the cinema.

"Why can't you let me take you in the evening in the car?" complained Peter when he heard of the plan. "It would be much quicker than going on that awful bus."

"It's very kind, my dear, but I want a day in Hinwood. There are heaps of things I need which I can't get in Overbridge."

"Such as — "

"Well — a tap washer — a pork pie — and a present for my aunt. Goodness, Peter, how you will argue! And there will be a mile-long queue tonight as well."

"I'd take the day off, only we're strawberry picking."

"I shouldn't let you. I never heard of such a thing. And I thought you had to spend every spare moment writing."

"So I do — only I can't write at night. I get so tired."

Loveday looked at him and saw that despite his tan there was a bluish tinge under his eyes and the corners of his mouth drooped.

It was a time which he often used for a purely social call. After he had finished his work on the farm he came back to the caravan, washed, ate an enormous meal and was then ready to talk to Loveday. But she, whose day had a different rhythm, was often at that time either cooking what she used to call dinner and now called supper, or doing some belated household chore, and although there were moments when she welcomed him, she frequently found him a nuisance.

He now sat back in a chair which came to be called his, and was apparently oblivious to the fact that Loveday did not want to see him. Perhaps it was because she was one of those people who find it almost impossible to be knowingly unkind. With a sigh she turned off the heat under the frying-pan, pushed the ironing to one side, went into the sitting-room, and sat down on the other side of the fireplace. It was as cold as November and he offered to light a fire.

'Oh dear," she thought, 'he is going to stay for hours.'

Aloud she said, putting on her glasses and reaching for the tapestry work she kept for moments which would be otherwise idle: "If you can't work in the evening, there's no reason why you should stop me."

She threaded a needle with wool.

"What has made you so lazy?"

"I don't know — farm work is tiring and I get sleepy, you know. I can write much better in winter, but I get up an hour earlier every day and I'm near the end at last. I wonder if it's any good."

"Don't you know?"

"Well, sometimes I read the beginning chapters and think its wonderful."

He laughed and fixed his legs on a convenient ledge on the fireplace, as if he had had it specially built for him.

"But most of the time," he went on, "I just have to make myself do it. And yet I like it, at least not so much doing it, but having done it. Does that sound crazy?"

"It does a bit," answered Loveday,

matching a strand of wool, "but it could be said about most achievements, from climbing a mountain to having a baby."

"You know, Loveday, you're the only person who cares about whether I finish it."

She frowned at the implied compliment, for she did not greatly care. She only realized that he needed encouragement and so she gave it and in doing so she found herself interested. There was something in her nature and experience which projected her into other people's lives and she was caught there. People called it friendship.

"You see," explained Peter, "it's a lonely sort of thing to do. No one can do it for me. No one can do it with me and it doesn't matter to anyone but me whether it is done at all."

"I'd like to be there when it's published."

"If, dear, if," laughed Peter. "Bless you Loveday, I can't think how I lived without you. I say, you haven't got a beer in the house, have you? I've got such a thirst."

She looked at him owl-like through the

spectacles she now wore for close work.

"I don't drink beer, and there's none in the house," she said. "There's some cider, I think. I'm not sure whether I gave it to Mr. Gorman when he fixed that tile."

He pulled a face.

"I expect it's flat," he said ungratefully. "I've got some beer in the caravan. I'll go and fetch it."

"No," said Loveday gently. "It's time you went home."

"Why, it's not ten o'clock. I'm enjoying myself, apart from the thirst, and I know where the tap is. I suppose I can have a drink of water before you throw me out, you inhospitable woman."

They both laughed. Neither of them had ever forgotten the bucket of water which Loveday had refused him. It served them as a joke for a long time.

She heard him fetch a glass from the cupboard and run the tap. He came back tinkling ice.

"I got some ice out of the fridge," he said calmly. "I like it iced."

Loveday was now used to the way he treated her cottage as if he had been born there. She realized that it was not familiarity, but something deeper that was characteristic of him. Like a young animal he made himself at once part of everywhere where he was happy or comfortable.

All she said was: "I hope you shut the fridge door properly."

He re-settled himself in his chair, drinking the water as if he had forgotten it was not the beer he wanted.

"Writing isn't a thing you can talk about," said Peter, proceeding to give the lie to his words by doing so.

The clock in the corner reminded them that it was now ten o'clock, but neither of them heard it.

★ ★ ★

It was after eleven before Loveday gathered her sewing put away her glasses and said severely: "I am now throwing you out, young man."

He knocked out his pipe with slow deliberation and began a delaying action like a child.

"I could go on all night," he complained.

"I don't feel a bit sleepy."

"I know, but I'm tired."

This statement was untrue; she was not in the least tired. The talk, the slight arguments that arose, the maddening egotism of youth had so stimulated her that she was alert and wide-eyed, but it was late and tomorrow was another day. She stood up and reluctantly he left his chair.

There was no rain, but a cold wind rushed through the trees and discouraged summer. Across the valley on the next hill shone the flootlit tower of Upper Spedding. As they stood in the doorway the light was extinguished.

"I'll take you there tomorrow," he said. "Teddy Livers went last night and said it looks wonderful from the other side of the valley. They've floodlit the pub as well, and the Church Farm. It's really the old Manor House. Old Teddy came back from his dart match there and said that cars were coming out all the evening from as far away as Hinwood."

"We shall be competing with London," laughed Loveday. "Well, if it's fine I'd like to go."

"Thank you kindly, sir," prompted Peter. "Talk about the manners of the older generation."

"Oh Peter, how rude I am."

She, who had been taken aback at the way he took everything for granted, realized now with compunction that perhaps her own manners were not a good example.

"All right," he said. "Tomorrow then. It isn't dark till about ten o'clock, is it? I want to do some writing first, so I'm not angling for supper."

"It would be no good if you were," laughed Loveday. "I shall have high tea at what Mrs. Spracker calls the 'Odium' Cafe — after having been to the Coronation."

"Film," amended Peter, and they both laughed.

'If Peter weren't here I don't believe I'd ever laugh,' thought Loveday, as she finally edged him through the back door and saw his torch flickering across the field. She drew the heavy bolt across and turned the old key. Crafers became a small, square fortress for the night.

Julian lunched every day with Bob Hindley, the solicitor, and Jimmy Lave, the auctioneer. They sat in the Three Tuns Hotel at a special table which was kept for them by an elderly but sprightly waitress, who saved them cuts off the joint long after other customers were told it was 'off', and knew that Jimmy hated sausages and Bob never ate cabbage.

At a quarter past one Julian came out of his office and walked across the Market Square, past Woolworth's and Guy's Stores, towards the dingy portals of the Three Tuns. He met old General Spears and his wife, the vicar, Miss Frant and Lucy Tripp and her mother, and, at the door of Boots', he met Loveday Flayne.

"All Overbridge," he said. "Are they giving something away? I've just seen all the people who sit in front of me at church — when I go," he added honestly.

"It's the film."

"What film?"

"The film of the Coronation."

"Oh yes, of course. I'm taking Johnny on Saturday."

"You'll never get in. Look at the queue."

Round the cinema wound an orderly mob and as they looked, two buses disgorged a straw-hatted crowd of boys from Hinwood Priory School.

"You're right. I shall have to revise my plans. Come and have some lunch with me. That is if you can eat it in three-quarters of an hour. I have a client at two o'clock."

He shot a wrist out of his cuff and inspected his watch. The invitation was not given with any enthusiasm and Loveday was pleased to be able to say that she had eaten her lunch very early and was about to join the queue. She almost saw him sigh with relief, and yet when he reached the table and saw that Bob and Jimmy were once more engaged in arguing about whether a brassie or an iron was the best club to use at the fourteenth, an argument which experience told him had no end, and also took away any appetite he might have, he thought of Loveday's refusal with faint regret.

158

"What veg?" asked Lily, the sprightly waitress, tapping her pencil against her teeth.

He had the sudden idea of asking Miss Flayne to come to Upper Spedding with him that evening when he took Ann and the children, as he had promised to do if it was fine, and he wondered if her telephone was connected yet.

"The joint's gorn but I've saved you a bit of heart," said Lily.

'Good old Lily,' thought Julian, and as Bob and Jim's argument showed no sign of abating, he turned *The Times* over to the crossword page.

* * *

By the time Loveday had seen the film and had tea the bus was full and she had to wait half an hour for the next one by the time she had reached Overbridge and walked up the hill to Crafers, her feet ached also.

She went through the familiar solitary ritual of returning home after a day's outing, she found the key, brought in the milk and paper, retrieved a loaf unhygienically perched in the coal shed, and gathered her letters from the mat. The house was chilly but stuffy, and as it was mercifully fine again, she opened the windows and sat down to read her mail.

After she had scanned the paper, picked some flowers and answered some letters she was filled with regret that she could not go peacefully to bed, but must, as she laughingly put it to herself, wait up for the flood-lighting! She almost wished she had asked Peter to supper. It would at any rate have kept her awake.

She could see no sign of life from the caravan and she pictured Peter inside writing his masterpiece, though he had, in actual fact, spent the evening playing shove ha'penny at the Duke's head.

★ ★ ★

A bang on the front door startled her for she seldom found occasion to open it, and as she drew the big bolts she wondered why Peter, who generally yelled at her from the gate and then opened the back door, should suddenly be so formal.

But it was not Peter. It was Julian,

flanked by Johnny and Roberta and followed by Ann.

"It will be a bit of a squash," he said, "but we wondered if you would like to come with us to see Upper Spedding floodlit."

"Do come in," said Loveday, and then was overwhelmed when they did so, as the sitting-room was not built for five. Before she could reply the crowd was augmented by Peter, who, though on speaking terms with the Lenhams, stood in the doorway and gave a greeting which was little more than a nod.

"It's awfully kind of you," said Loveday, "but Peter is taking me."

"Well, we can all go," said Julian. "Look, Miss Flayne, you come with us and Peter can take Ann and the children — "

Thus lightly did Julian divide the generations, and the 'children' all gave loud acclamation to the plan because Peter's car was open. By the time fears had occured to Julian that Johnny might catch cold, the plans were too far under way to be altered; Ann and Roberta were squabbling as to who should sit in the front and Ann was voicing her joy that she had a head-scarf in her pocket. No one noticed that Peter said nothing. His passengers had all embarked and still he stood in the doorway without moving.

"You'd better go on in front, my lad," said Julian, "because I've got to turn round. Anyhow, I don't doubt you drive much too fast and will be there before I've got into top gear."

Peter looked at Loveday with his eyes darkened by temper. He had been cautioned for speeding by the police and Loveday thought it was unlucky that Julian should have mentioned his fast driving.

"I expect a closed car will be better for you," was all he said, looking only at Loveday, and turned on his heel. There was a roar as he shot the corner, his passengers all waving.

Julian was less hurried. He watched Loveday hide the key and then walked slowly after her up the path. The lupins glowed in the half dark, for they were good this year, and more by luck than design there was a small bed by the gate of self-set Russells. Julian stopped to admire them.

"You must have worked very hard," he said.

"Oh, I have — I do — " said Loveday. "Book in hand. There are some nice things which I am gradually disentangling from the jungle, though I knew nothing about gardening, but it comes back to me a bit and I am learning. We lived in a countrified suburb until I grew up and my mother was a great gardener. I have only just realized the anguish it must have been to leave her garden and go to live in Kensington."

"Would you go back?" he asked.

"I don't know. There are things I miss, concerts, the ballet, those funny little exhibitions of pictures, oh, lots of things. Most of all the impersonalness of it. I can't easily get used to the violence of my neighbour's interest."

"One can be anonymous in London, I agree."

"The way they put odd facts together and concoct an incorrect story," went on Loveday, "but then I'm getting just as bad. I see Mr. Livers in his tidy clothes

163

at eight o'clock inspecting his calves. It's market day and I know, or I think I know, that he is going to sell them."

"And from that it's easy to invent the price he got."

"Exactly, if I had half an idea of how much a calf would fetch — "

"Probably about seven or eight pounds."

"Really? You see, I learn all the time."

"Still, I take it you like living here?"

"Oh yes."

He did not know why this answer pleased him and as he opened the gate Upper Spedding, four miles away on the next hilltop, became suddenly magnificent.

"Comic to think it's done by pressing a switch," said Julian. "Have you been to London to see the lights?"

"No, I suppose I shall have to go," said Loveday, as they drove down the lane and across the main road. "I wonder if it will be more beautiful than Upper Spedding."

She laughed.

"I can see you are becoming one of us," he said.

"Were you born here?"

"Not in Overbridge. My father came from the other side of the county, but I had an uncle in practice in Hinwood. Frances and I were born in India and we lived all over the place until I qualified. I bought Friar's House because it was ridiculously cheap and Frances and I liked it, then she went to America and the war was on. Poor Judy, my wife, loathed it. I made her keep it because it was a safe area and you couldn't get anything in those day. Remember?"

Loveday remembered. The war years, separated from the present by a slab of uneasy peace, had memories of gaiety which made one overlook in retrospect the bombs and shortages and all the anxieties and misery.

"Were you in it?" she asked.

"Yes, I was in the infantry, but I was in England quite a bit before I went to North Africa and then on to Italy. I — I was there when my wife was killed."

"That must have been terrible."

She pictured him broken-hearted, alone. So deliberate was he about everything that they had still not started before he answered. He saw that she was comfortable, shut the car door, turned the ignition key and Loveday wished she had not spoken on such a tricky subject.

Julian was an honest man and he always hated people thinking he was bereft when Judy died. His conscience was nagged by the fact that he had found married life less happy than people supposed. No one could imagine that anyone who possessed Judy, with her vital beauty, her vivid intelligence, her quicksilver charm, could be in a state that fell short of bliss. But even after years had dulled the sharpness of the memory, Julian remembered her temper, which was unpredictable and, when fairly under weigh, uncontrollable. He remembered her unending criticism, not only of him, but of everybody, the unkind curl of her lip as she tore away one's pride in oneself, however small it might be. All her gaiety, all her tinkling laughter, for she had been what people are pleased to call 'amusing', did not ease the sting of the other memories.

The only thing he completely forgot was her unfaithfulness. Somehow, on looking back, that seemed less important. He drove on to the field gate to turn and when he spoke at last it was to say:

"The kids were a problem — still are. Johnny was a poor peaked thing. Luckily Ann's grandparents took her over, and I can't say I like her grandmother. I don't think she has brought up Ann in quite the right way and yet I can't see what else I could have done, she's not my child but she's fonder really of us, I do believe. Of course I should never have managed at all if it hadn't been for Marcy. She was wonderful. She came to Friar's House and looked after Johnny and a whole lot of landgirls they billeted on her and so I was able to go back and finish off the war."

"And you had Friar's House to come back to?"

"Yes. You know the chaps used to sing that song: 'You'd be so nice to come home to'? I used to think of Friar's House. I suppose you were in the Services?"

"No. You see at the beginning I did typing for my father, very badly, but I improved. Then as things went on his work became rather important and I felt I was being useful there and I had exemption, which was an awfully good thing, as mother was terribly ill for six months before she died and I was able to nurse her. Of course we had no help by then. It really was rather hard work. After she died in 1946 I went to South Africa with my father. He ought never to have gone. He was too old, but he was a year younger than Winston Churchill and no one could make him stop while Winston still functioned. On the boat coming back he had a slight stroke. Everyone was terribly kind, the ship's doctor was marvellous, but it was horrible — horrible — "

Loveday's mind went back to the grey days when she watched the sharp brilliance of her father's brain dulled gradually to mediocrity, all his moods and tantrums merged into a quiet meekness.

"I wasn't really sorry when he died. He found life such a dismal burden towards the end."

By the time they reached Upper Spedding they found themselves sobered by thoughts into which their conversation had led them and they were unprepared for the gay scene. Cars were drawn up along what Upper Spedding called the 'Bottom Road'. The darkness was alive with voices and flashes of lights. Above on the hill glowed the church, and Rose Inn, and, slightly on the left, the Manor Farm, all brought out of their obscurity by the searching brilliance of the flood-lighting.

The red car was not hard to find, but it was empty.

"I suppose they are all right," said Loveday uneasily.

"Bound to be," murmured Julian. "Shall we get out and go across the road? That's where all the people are, so I imagine there's a reason."

It was closing time and the Rose Inn was inhospitably ejecting its clientele. Farewells sounded across the little street, doors opened and shut. The inhabitants of Upper Spedding, a sparse and spreading parish, who had seen the flood-lighting on the first night and were no longer interested, now looked resentfully at the parked cars. Somewhere Julian could hear Ann's voice and then a chorus of 'Daddy — Uncle Julian' brought them prominence in the crowd. Johnny and Roberta appeared from under their elbows.

"Here we are. Isn't this fun? I wish they did it all the time," said Johnny, jumping up and down.

Roberta refused to be impressed. Under her patronizing gaze Upper Spedding flood-lighting became a patriotic attempt at something beyond its scope. Peter walked to a gate in the low wall, and leapt over it; Loveday could just see the familiar hunch of his shoulder. She wondered what had happened to Ann until she heard her voice across the road talking excitedly to half a dozen people, all with their backs to the flood-lighting.

"Do you suppose Johnny will remember this?" said Loveday.

"Do you suppose that we shall?"

"That's different, I mean, don't you think that illumination will become so much more commonplace that there won't be enough dark by contrast?"

They began to discuss the flatness of the lighting, how it took away all depths, and from there they touched on three-dimensional films, the first talkies, the silent films. They were the same generation, they remembered the same things, and they were far away in that space of time between the wars when they had grown up.

"All my conversation with the children starts: 'When I was a boy,'" said Julian.

"I wouldn't be young again."

"Wouldn't you? I thought women hated getting older."

"Perhaps we do, but all the same I'm very glad I haven't got to be twenty-four again."

She looked along the wall to Peter who had now turned and was looking across at them, and to Ann walking on with the small mob she had joined.

"One has all the time one wants when one is young, but no patience," she went on. "And now we have patience but less time."

Julian thought this statement over hours later when he lay wakeful at Friar's House, but at Upper Spedding, as Loveday spoke with that slow half-reflecting manner which he found so congenial, Roberta and Johnny appeared, obviously about to have one of their sudden quarrels with which Julian hated to deal.

"They're tired," he apologized.

Loveday put her hand on Johnny's shoulder and he shivered.

"You know he's cold."

"So am I," said Roberta. "I'm freezing."

"They'll have to come home with us. That open car will give them pneumonia."

"Oh no," they protested. "We're boiling really."

"Enough of this," said Julian. "Where are the others?"

Ann could still be seen, but Peter had disappeared, and while Julian took the children and turned the car Loveday walked up the road to look for him. He came out from behind the trees at the entrance to the farm with an expression of glumness which Loveday had come to know well. Everything about him seemed to droop with the corners of his mouth.

All this she ignored, saying cheerfully, "It's remarkable how the light beautifies that old farm."

He stood with his back to the buildings, a black pigmy.

"Fancy landing me with that bunch of kids," he said.

"So that's what has annoyed you. Don't be childish, Peter. I thought you'd be happy with Ann."

"Well, I wasn't. She has absolutely nothing to say and looks at you as if she thinks there's something perverted about you if you don't make love to her at once."

"Peter, don't be so outrageous," said Loveday, genuinely shocked. Then she laughed: "And with Roberta and Johnny in the back, how could she have had any such idea?"

"I tell you, she had no other idea. I'm not going to drive her home."

"Oh but you must, Peter. It would be so rude."

"Rude? Who's being rude? Didn't I ask you to come out with me and you just jump into another car with another chap and leave me to cope with a lot of kids and a horrible piece like Ann?"

"I — I did no such thing — "

Then she reflected that this statement

173

was true, leaving out the horribleness of Ann, with which she could not agree.

"I thought you just wanted to see the flood-lighting," she said in a chastened voice.

"Well, I didn't I'd seen it. I wanted to show it to you. I — I thought you'd like it."

"But I do. It's wonderful."

They both stood looking at the crisp outlines of the farm with the church beyond, and as they did so an unseen hand put out the lights. There was suddenly nothing in the velvet dark but themselves.

"It was sweet of you to bring me," said Loveday.

"I didn't bring you," objected Peter.

"Oh, dear, please don't go on."

She laughed because it had become ridiculous and suddenly he laughed too, and as he laughed the invisible tight band, which was always laid across Loveday's head at the hint of a quarrel with anyone at all from a rude porter to a lover, was removed.

Julian was standing by his car looking anxiously for Ann. By now the fact that

Roberta and Johnny's bedtime had long been passed was painfully apparent, and they were both having a boasting match which, Julian knew, would end in tears. He could see Peter and Loveday coming towards him, but where was Ann? The block of cars thinned to three and a voice said:

"I say, you're Mr. Lenham, aren't you? I was to tell you that Ann has gone back with Gordon Camber."

"Oh — indeed — has she?" said Julian.

He did not know who Gordon Camber was and he had, as always, a vague feeling that he should protest, but he was not sure why. He sighed thankfully when he saw Loveday.

"I'm sorry," he said to Peter, "but you've lost all your passengers. The children are cold — "

Chorus of 'No, we aren't.'

"The children are cold," repeated Julian, "and when I say they're cold they'd better be — and Ann has gone."

Peter said nothing but 'Oh!' and looked at Loveday, who was by now in the front seat of Julian's car adjusting the window.

"Sorry," said Julian again.

"It doesn't signify," said Peter, who liked to use an eighteenth century turn of speech when he wished to be particularly icy. This Julian did not appreciate and merely thought the annoying boy was a mixture of toughness and affectation.

There was a bang and a clang and a roar and the red car was gone. Julian started his own car almost imperceptibly by contrast, but by the time he dropped Loveday at her gate the only sign of Peter was an eye of light across the field.

9

The Invalid

MARCY had asked Loveday to supper at Christmas Farm, with instructions to catch the evening bus from the Molesworth turning on the main road. She was to be brought back by some other guests who lived on the far side of Overbridge. It was a fine night, though still cold for June, and as Loveday walked down the lane with her high-heeled shoes in a bag and a lace scarf across her hair, she had a momentary feeling that she was a child again. The shoebag brought a mental flashback of dressing for a party by the nursery fire, with extra vests and admonitions as to good behaviour. Her life at Crafers was so much simpler and happier than she ever remembered, that it gave her a sensation of physical well-being. She pictured herself ending her days at Crafers as an energetic spinster.

'Isn't she wonderful?' people would say, as they did of old Miss Trant. 'Eighty-three and walks to church.' She smiled to herself at the thought as she came to the end of the lane, *her* lane.

"Hullo, Loveday," called a voice.

It was Peter coming across the road from the telephone box.

"Loveday, I say, I am sorry about last night. I was awfully rude."

The apology was so unexpected that she became willing to admit imperfections in her own behaviour.

"I was rude too," she said. "Let's forget all about it."

"It may have been because I felt so ghastly. I still do. I've just been phoning the Duke's Head to say I simply can't play in the darts match."

"Then you must be ill," laughed Loveday. "Have you got a cold?"

"I suppose so."

"Well, go to bed and take some aspirin. Have you any?"

"No."

"Look, I am going to supper with the Lowesmores. There are some aspirins in the bathroom cupboard and a thermometer, You know where the key is. Take your temperature and go to bed. You oughtn't to have come out."

"Oh, for pity's sake don't fuss."

"Very well. I only meant to be kind."

"So you are, very kind, only I loathe being pampered."

Loveday looked at him and saw that he was flushed. At the same moment he shivered and complained that he was frozen.

"My dear boy, do go to bed and stay in the warm."

"All right, only don't call me a boy."

★ ★ ★

It was after eleven when she returned. The evening had been unexpectedly congenial; she was now pleasantly fatigued and looking forward to the comfort of sleep. She had put the milk for her bed-time drink on to boil when her eye fell on note by the clock.

Many thanks for the aspirins. My temperature seems to be 103°. I washed the thermometer and put it back.

                              Peter.

She drew aside the curtains to know if Peter was still awake and saw a glow of light in the corner of the field. After a moment of indecision she put the milk in a Thermos flask, filled a hot-water bottle and stuffed it in a basket with a cushion to keep it hot. As she thrust her feet into her rubber boots she accomplished the total wreck of her nylons.

The field was muddy, but in the past few months a path had been worn across it between the caravan and Crafers. She tapped lightly on the door.

"It's only me, Loveday. Are you all right?"

There was no answer at first, and then she heard a bump as he rolled over in his bunk and hit the side of the caravan.

"Oh, Loveday, bless you," he called. "The door is unlocked."

She pushed it open.

"It's all in an awful mess."

Peter waved a hand at the dishes piled in the tiny sink, his mackintosh in a heap on the floor. He half-lay on the bunk, dressed, and covered in a rug, but as he spoke his teeth chattered.

180

"What's up with you?" inquired Loveday.

"Lord knows — " his voice was strangely hoarse.

"Oughtn't you to be in bed?"

"Sounds silly, Loveday," he said in a half-whisper, "but I can't manage it. I did try to undress but I fell over."

"I'll help you."

"You can't."

"Of course I can. You'd be more comfortable. Are you hungry?"

He shut his eyes.

She felt his pulse. It raced unevenly; his hand was hot and damp, yet he shivered and said he was frozen. She put the hot-water bottle by his side and he turned over and cuddled it without speaking.

"We must warm you up somehow. Let me help you undress and then we'll roll you in the blankets. I've brought you a hot drink."

He turned and looked at her: "Do you mind? I feel so miserable."

She found his pyjamas and warmed them, helped him off with his shirt and laughed as she tugged off his trousers

181

and pants and covered him quickly with warm blankets.

"I'm horribly embarrassed. What a thing," he said; but he admitted he was warmer and sipped the milk gratefully.

"Haven't you any more blankets?"

"No."

"I'll have to fetch you some. Where's your duffel coat?"

She found it and piled it on him.

When she went back to Crafers for the blankets she picked up the thermometer. He was nearly asleep when she returned, but he opened his mouth meekly for her to take his temperature. It registered just over 104°.

"Is it still up?" he asked.

"Just a bit."

"I ache so."

She hung up his clothes and thought swiftly. There were two doctors in the village, she did not remember their names. It was now nearly midnight and a quick glance in the direction of the Livers farm which showed no light confirmed her assumption they were in bed. There was nothing for it but to walk to the main road, ring up someone and find a doctor, but who? The Vicar? Julian Lenham? She remembered a complaint of Julian's that no one at Friar's House went to bed early, and she hurried back to her cottage to collect some coppers for the telephone. It was a quarter of a mile to the box and not for the first time Loveday cursed the lack of telephone. She was, it seemed, 'on the waiting list', and although she told herself such isolation was restful, on occasions like this she composed rude letters to the Postmaster General. By the last flicker of her rebellious torch she found the number.

"Overbridge 24," she asked hopefully.

Julian sounded so put out at Loveday's request for the name of the doctor that Loveday caught the tired inflexion in his voice, and she regretted her impulse and thought too late that she could have asked the police or even the telephone exchange. She did not know that Landon's friend, K.K., was once again proposing to occupy his bed, and he found the prospect of a night on the sofa uninviting.

"I'm terribly sorry. I hope you hadn't gone to bed."

"No. I was just taking out the dog. Look, I'll tell you what. The Hoves only left here ten minutes ago and I can see the light in their house. They live just across the road, you know. I'll nip and ask him to come up to you. Anything else I can do?"

He made the offer, but Loveday felt he would be relieved if it were not taken seriously. Thanking him she rang off and pushed her way out of the box on to the dark road. There was no moon, the sky was clear and star-dusted and all around her was the scent of summer. Any thought of sleep had gone.

★ ★ ★

When the doctor's car drew up she heard voices, and one of them was Julian's.

"I brought Dr. Hove in my car. He had a flat tyre and thought you'd be glad not to wait."

"Indeed I am," said Loveday. "How very good of you both to come so quickly. It's across the field, you know." She turned to Julian. "Would you like to wait here?"

184

"No thanks. I'll stay in the car. You won't be all night, Tom, I hope."

Tom Hove ejected himself from the car with the breathless energy of the large man. With unhurried calm he retrieved his bag from the back, felt his pockets for his stethoscope and laid his hand across his heart to assure himself that his throat-torch, pen, diary and thermometer bulged his breast pocket. Loveday led the way across her garden and out into the field where Peter's light showed the caravan against the trees.

They were a long time. Julian lit a cigarette and walked round the car to stretch his legs. It was always chilly on the top of the hill and he shivered, looking down at the village and watching the few late lights snuff out one by one until all was dark behind the trees. He finished his cigarette and, after an impatient pause, he lit another. With relief he heard the voices of Loveday and the doctor as they walked towards him, and he put his hand out to pull the starter, repenting of his kindness and wishing he were home, when Tom Hove bent his head to the car window.

"See here, Julian, we've got to move this boy. Do you think you could take your car down the lane to the gate and across the field?"

"What price my springs?"

"Oh, to hell with your springs. It's quite a decent track, the boy uses it anyway."

"I'm just going into the house for blankets," said Loveday.

"She says," said Tom Hove, indicating Loveday's departing figure, "that she'll look after him. He's got pneumonia. I'll be half the night getting him into hospital, because I know Hinwood General is packed out. I've been trying to fix in an emergency all day. Dam' scandal. Anyway, she says she'll cope and you and I can lift him out and wrap him up. He's pretty ill. I'm afraid you'll have to run me back to the surgery for some sulphanilamide.

★ ★ ★

Julian groaned as the car bumped over the ruts.

"I hadn't bargained on any of this,"

he said. "We'll be all night."

"Make you realize the benefits of the health service, and do you know, this idiot has never even bothered to register."

His grumbles rumbled on.

"Decent sort of creature," said Julian. "Who?"

"The Flayne woman. Says she nursed pneumonia twice before. Kind, I must admit. Comic little caravan. Here we are."

The eye which Peter showed was not welcoming, but the two older men treated him like a troublesome child and he was too ill to protest. By the time they had wrapped him up he was also too exhausted to talk.

"We've got to be quick," said Tom Hove. "Unless we are, moving him will be worse than leaving him here alone."

They were so swift that Loveday had barely time to make up the bed.

"It's always aired there because of the hot-water tank," she said. She had lit an electric fire and the small room under the eaves looked cheerfully feminine with its shining chintz frills and glazed gay colours.

While they were gone to get the prescribed tablets, Loveday moved quietly round the room, making sure that she had forgotten nothing, while Peter lay dozing, apparently unconscious of her presence. She turned out the light and left him, leaving the door ajar and the light shining in from the landing.

"Loveday," came from the bed. "Are you going away?"

"I'll be quite near. I shall hear you. You are having some tablets as soon as they come."

"Sorry I'm such a bore."

"That's all right."

She did not deny that the upheaval was causing her trouble. It was the kind of thing she thought she had foresworn when she left London.

"Try and go to sleep, my dear," was all she said.

"It hurts so to move," he complained. She went back into the room and tried to make him comfortable, but he moaned at each movement and then lay back, sweating and trying not to cough. He clutched her fingers and she left them in his hand. She was reminded by the glow from the electric fire, which was the only light, of childhood illnesses, jelly, puzzles, and the calm presence of her mother. When Julian returned she was still there.

"I let old Tom go to bed," he explained. "He is expecting a maternity case and he wanted to fix his tyre in case he gets another call tonight. The lad must take two now, then every four hours, and Tom will come again tomorrow and get on to Nurse Jones, District Nurse, you know, fierce woman. She'll blanket bath him within an inch of his life, I don't doubt."

Loveday thanked him and heard his car door shut. She wished she had offered him a whisky-and-soda or a cup of tea, for she had found his kindness a comfort.

"Who was that?" asked Peter, with a fretful edge on his voice.

"Only Mr. Lenham with your tablets. Here they are, you take two now."

"I can't swallow pills."

"Nonsense," said Loveday briskly.

"Don't be fierce, Loveday."

"I have to be," said Loveday, thinking

of Nurse Jones. She had a sudden thought. "You aren't going to be silly about bedpans and things, are you?"

She was relieved to find that this part of the nursing he considered to be a joke and it was Loveday who was embarrassed. She set the clock for half-past four, took off her best grey dress, looking regretfully at a milk splash on the sleeve, examined her face in the mirror. Tiredness made her a present of ten years. She grimaced and turned thankfully to her bed. Ten minutes later, so it seemed, the alarm rang.

10

The Nurse

LOVEDAY whisked an egg into some milk and hoped that she could persuade Peter to drink it. Two days had gone by and he had eaten nothing. Vague slogans about 'keeping the strength up' occurred to her as she turned the handle of the egg-beater, but apart from not eating he was a good patient, lying quietly in a dose, only half aware of where he was. The District Nurse had roused him briskly with a blanket bath and the day had been so busy for Loveday that she was surprised to hear the bells ringing below in the village for the evening service. She had forgotten it was Sunday.

The smallness of the cottage made her afraid to turn on her wireless set in case it should disturb Peter and when she came in from the garden where she had been weeding under his window while the light faded, she was chilled for a moment by the stillness. She shook the thought that Peter might die out of her mind, and as he refused the egg with the grimace of a small boy, she slipped her arm under his head and fed him spoonful by spoonful, wiping his aggressive, stubbly chin with a napkin. He seemed almost unaware of her, gave a gasp and a groan as he lay down again and was lost in some limbo of fever.

His temperature showed no signs of dropping, in spite of the tablets, and Loveday knew that there were people who were resistant to them. She began to wonder about his mother in Australia. All she knew about her was that she had re-married and she did not even know her new name. The night before she had had almost no sleep, for she was awakened relentlessly every four hours and only slept again with difficulty half an hour before the next dose was due, but she was not yet unduly fatigued, for she was small and energetic, and after six months of freedom she found a certain satisfaction in doing a necessary job well. She knew, however, that if this went on she would soon tire, so she lit a cigarette and lay back in a chair with her feet on Miss Cox's beaded footstool. The evening was warm, the front door was open and she looked across her new flower-beds to the lane. It led by a roundabout way to the Livers' farm and nowhere else, and one could derive a simple form of amusement from the occasional car which took a wrong turning, was forced into a difficult piece of backing and then turned by the field gate. Otherwise all was still as the twilight faded.

It would soon be time for another dose for Peter.

As Loveday rose from her chair the gate clicked, a dog ran up the path, followed by Julian.

"I wondered," he said, "if there was anything we could do."

He came in, scraping his head on the lintel, and lowered himself into a chair.

"That's very kind."

"Not really," said Julian, "because I wanted a walk."

"Not up this hill," laughed Loveday. "I am now used to the idea that no one comes up the hill without good reason."

"Well, I have a good reason. I want to know how the boy is."

"Not any better."

"I am sorry. Actually, as Ann would say, I knew that too. I meet Tom at lunch time. Do you know, as much as anything I wanted to get away from everyone in the house."

Loveday opened the cigarette box and handed it to him while he continued: "It's appalling. Ann and K.K. dancing in the hall, Roberta and Johnny playing circus, Frances and Landon quarrelling, well, not quarrelling, but just talking to each other with louder voice than usual and an edge on them. Landon has had to stay in England longer than he expected, I think he loves us less than he did. Do you know what I mean?"

Loveday nodded.

"Why did I have to live in a house that is about as peaceful as Hampstead Heath on Easter Monday?" he went on. "It would have been all right without this K.K."

"You know," said Loveday, handing

him a sherry, "I haven't any idea who K.K. is."

"He came after our party and when they'd drunk my entire cellar dry, that is to say what gin was over, and I thought they really would go to bed, he produced a bottle out of his bag and it went on and on."

"Why didn't you go to bed?"

"How could I? I was sleeping on the sofa and K.K. and Landon were discussing the Taft Hartley Law on it. He has been twice since. I've broken a spring in the sofa. How peaceful you look."

"If I do, it's misleading, because I assure you I've been running round soothing fevered brows and administering doses for what seems like a life-time."

"Have you? I'm sorry. It's decent of you to take the boy in."

"Mrs. Spracker already suspects the worst. I never thought of people being so stupid — me at my great age — "

"Country people's minds are direct and simple and you don't look any great age."

She was sitting erect in Miss Cox's

other easy chair, trim in brown linen slacks and a scarlet shirt, her neat ankles hidden in scarlet socks. The shadows took away the years from her face and he saw only the good bones, the straight small nose, the mouth with the sideways smile. He wondered idly how old she was.

"My mother stayed forty until she was fifty," said Loveday, "and then fifty until she was sixty. After that she was proud of wearing well."

He decided she was probably a few years younger than he was.

Peter called and she rose lightly from the chair and ran up the stairs which led up from the sitting-room. He could hear her walking round and the soft buzzing of voices. When she came down her face was serious.

"I wish you'd come and look at him. His temperature just seems to stay up. It's still 103°. I thought with these new drugs it should come down with a bang."

Julian found himself looking at a huddle of bedclothes. Peter opened his eyes, gave Julian a blank stare, closed them again, and murmured that it was time to go to Livers, they were thrashing and he said he'd help them.

"Tomorrow," said Loveday gently, pulling the sheets straight. He clutched her hand.

"Tomorrow," he said, and his voice had a croak in it. He didn't appear to have noticed Julian, who stood looking at him in silence before moving on to the small landing between the two bedrooms.

"Don't go away," said Peter to Loveday.

"I'll come back. I have to go downstairs for a little while. Try to sleep again."

He did not answer except with a small child-like sound and Loveday gently released her fingers. She left the door ajar and downstairs they talked in whispers while Julian stood reluctantly prepared to leave.

"He looks a bad colour," he said.

"Yes — sort of blue-grey. Dr. Hove came this morning and I hardly like to bother him again, but I feel so responsible."

She pulled nervously at the collar of her shirt while the dog danced amongst their feet. The hard light of electricity which she switched on in the hall and porch showed the pallor and tiredness which the kind twilight had hidden, yet there was a resolution about her which made men, while wishing to protect her, realize that she could manage quite well without them. She pushed her hands through her tractable hair. It stood up at the back in an unlovely but likeable manner.

"When you get home," she said, "I wonder if you would be so kind as to ring Dr. Hove and tell him about Peter and see what he says. I don't like to leave the house to go to the telephone and I don't want to bother the doctor unnecessarily."

"Of course, with pleasure. I feel anxious for you — indeed, about you."

He held out his hand in farewell, oddly formal.

"Do you? There's no need, but you've been a comforting visitor."

The resolution disappeared, she gave a small defenceless smile. Julian, who had intended to call on Tom and tell him about Peter in any case, felt annoyed with himself for not speaking first. A ridiculous desire to protect this woman invaded his heart, yet even as he looked at her it passed, for he knew she did not need it. She was self-sufficient, capable and obviously happy, as if she had come to terms with middle-age. As he walked down the hill he thought: 'I do enjoy being with her, and yet I never remember her clearly except the grey streak in her hair, and those light grey eyes.'

* * *

Tom rattled his stethoscope and looked through his glasses at a Carrington Bowles print of Vauxhall Gardens on the wall of the sitting-room. Suddenly he turned and faced Loveday with a frown.

"He seems to have a resistance to the drug. We'll have to try something else. By the way, hasn't he got any people?"

"You mean, they ought to be sent for?"

"We — ell, shall we see how he is in the morning?"

"His mother is in Australia, his father is dead and she married again. I don't even know her name. The parson might. I believe he knew something about them."

"I should ask him — in case."

"Yes — I will — but it's all rather difficult. You see I can't leave here and I have no telephone."

"I didn't realize you had no telephone. I'll send a message to the Vicar to come and see you. You're all right, aren't you? Shall I try to get him moved? It would be better really not to disturb him, if you can manage."

"I'm all right for a bit. I'll see if I can get Mrs. Spracker to give me a hand tomorrow, because if I can get a modicum of sleep I can manage for a long time."

"As a rule it's only a day or two and then the temperature drops."

"I know, that's what I thought."

"That would be easy, but it will be more than that. We've evidently got more trouble on our hands than we thought."

He gave a comfortable laugh. Birth, death and the ardours of nursing were nothing to him. He looked at Loveday and sized her up medically, clear eyes, calm manner, good digestion, he thought, healthy blood stream, straight back, must be forty. She would do what she had to do until it was ended. He also noticed that she had small, neat feet and long, slender legs swinging gracefully from narrow hips. He nodded goodbye.

★ ★ ★

While Loveday ate her breakfast she closed her eyes for a moment and suddenly was lost in drowsiness. She shook it from her and drank more coffee. During the night she had not slept at all. When she was not creeping into Peter's room to see why he was groaning and struggling and carelessly playing with the bedclothes, she was making hot drinks, filling hot-water bottles, administering the tablets at four-hourly intervals. Now at last they seemed to be having some effect for Peter's temperature had dropped a little. It was 102° and he was asleep.

She carried her dirty dishes to the sink and began half-heartedly the chores for the day — the boiler — a quick flick round. Mrs. Spracker was not due until the end of the week, but when the baker came he would take a message. Loveday dared not leave the house even to walk as far as the farm, and soon she would need reinforcements for the larder. The thought of the trivial workings of the daily round, more pyjamas for Peter, eggs from somewhere, Brand's Essence, Ovaltine, barley water, the laundry day, fluttered like birds in her brain. She opened the back door and drank in the air blowing across the valley from the sea. The trees were heavy with summer foliage. The caravan, without Peter's coming and going, clanking of pails, which she found so irritating, looked sadly deserted. She felt alone and apprehensive. Eagerly she listened for sounds in the lane — the Vicar — the doctor, Mrs. Livers. No one came, but at last the baker brought news of the outside world. Mrs. Spracker had had to go over to see her Dolly who had scalded her foot and she said could Miss Flayne manage. She'd be up next Friday as usual.

Loveday took a loaf warm and unhygienic from the baker's hands, discussed Peter's illness with him, and heard about the time when he was in hospital with a poisoned hand. She felt as if she were stranded in a desert and being fed by parachuted food. I must ask Mrs. Livers for some eggs, she thought. She went back into the house momentarily revived and discovered that two hours, she knew not how, had vanished, and it was now once more time for Peter to take his tablets.

He was awake but he had a drugged look, as if a film lay over his senses.

She propped his head as he swallowed the pills.

"Anything else I can do?"

"No thank you. Not even the old bedpan," he gave a grin.

He lay back, his head still imprisoning her hand. She did not move and he turned his face and lay for a moment with his cheek on her palm. His face was still a bluish-grey round the lips, cyanosed, the doctor said, and Loveday wondered again about his mother. Should she say: 'How can I get hold of your mother?' In the few months they had been neighbours she had learnt to know so little of him that she could table the facts. He had been in the Malayan Police until he had dysentery; he was trying to write a book and was doing farm work to make a living while he did so; his mother had married again and lived in Australia; he didn't care about his stepfather, and he had a younger sister. It was incredible how little she knew, considering that he had gradually progressed from scattered meetings, usually acrimonious, to a daily call.

She had never really considered his face. There was his scornful look, then his endearing grin, which came and vanished so quickly one might miss it altogether and remember only the scorn. She looked down at him now, noticed for the first time his mouth, a sensitive clear-cut upper lip with a fuller lower lip, slightly sensuous. His jutting narrow chin was covered in stubble and it pricked her hand. He had been too weak to shave himself and the nurse was not coming till tomorrow. She moved her hand and smoothed back his hair which he always grew longer than Loveday thought desirable and which now stuck out in lint-coloured peaks. He opened his eyes again and gave her his fleeting grin.

"Those ribbons you used to talk about. I'll need them," he said, and closed his eyes again.

It seemed very hot under the low ceiling and she opened the second little window. Downstairs the rooms had an unloved look as if all life were concentrated on the invalid. For the first time since she had left London she longed for someone to talk to — anyone. Looking at the cherished view and the far-away chimneys of the farm she regretted her isolation.

★ ★ ★

As she was washing up the lunch things the parson stooped his way into the kitchen. "I'm terribly sorry I couldn't call before. I had a wedding. What can I do for you? Tom Hove left a message for me to come quickly. Are you in any trouble?"

"Not me. It's Peter Colefield."

She shut the kitchen door so that their voices should not carry up the stairs which led from the sitting-room. The Vicar sat on the only chair and Loveday perched herself on a high stool by the

205

sink. She had a momentary feeling of being in a cocktail bar, which faded at the sight of the unwashed dishes.

"He's ill I hear, and you're looking after him," said the Vicar, removing his cycling clips.

"Yes, he's quite bad, I'm afraid, and I realize I know nothing about him. I wondered if — if he should get worse, whether you knew how to find his mother. I believe she married again."

"No, I don't know. All I know is that he was in Yorkshire working for my brother and found it too bleak and Charles gave him a letter of introduction to me and I spoke to the Livers and he came. I know nothing at all about him, except that his people are in Australia. Do you think they should be told?"

"I don't know. The doctor said he'd come early this afternoon and by then we'd know if the tablets were acting. He does seem a bit better to me, but I'm sure his mother would want to be here."

"How long does it take from Australia? Three days by plane? Or is it longer? By that time he'd be either better — or — dead."

Loveday shivered. She had nursed her father and mother. It was by no means the first time she had been close to death — and Peter was almost a stranger to her. But she had a swift composite picture of his grin and his rudeness and his clanking buckets and loud laugh, and tears came into her eyes.

"He must have friends, everyone has a friend of some sort, even the most lonely," said the Vicar.

"Oh, he has — at least there was a young couple who came down to see him a while ago — " Loveday remembered the noise they had made, "but they were Australians. You see he hasn't been in England so very long. He said Australia is no place to write a book."

"Well, of course, if the worst came to the very worst we could always get on to Australia House."

"Yes," said Loveday bleakly, uncomforted.

"Shall I go and see him?"

She wondered why she associated the parson with death, and as she saw his black cassock go up the stairs with the frayed edges of grey flannel trousers appearing surprisingly above army boots as the skirts of his cassock moved, she thought that he looked like a harbinger of death. He came down almost immediately and said in a cheerful whisper:

"Asleep — didn't like to disturb him."

Loveday was making some tea.

"Do you mind having it in the kitchen? I don't want to make a noise and the cottage is so small."

The parson drank his tea with relieved sighs and Loveday suddenly realized that visiting sick strangers was not perhaps a congenial occupation, unless one was a born busybody. She asked after his children and how the fund for preventing the church tower form collapsing was progressing.

"We want a thousand pounds, and we've got two hundred and forty-two pounds. Two hundred and forty-two pound, thirteen and ninepence to precise. Splendid, isn't it?"

The simplicity of his optimism touched Loveday. She made some excuse about not going to church and it sounded lame.

"I'll write to Charles and see if I can find out something for you," said the Vicar, "but I daresay by the time we get any information it won't be needed, or too late — " he said.

"Did you think he looked very ill?"

"Bad colour — bad colour. Have you got any help?"

"Nurse Jones came in yesterday and I think she is coming tomorrow. I should be perfectly all right if I had Mrs. Spracker or the telephone."

"Oh yes, Mrs. Spracker is a great stand-by, but I hear she has had to go over to Spedding to see that daughter of hers."

"There's no one else, I suppose?"

He shook his head.

"The number of times I'm asked for a daily woman, you'd think I was an employment agency. Do you think I should go round asking people if they were saved?" he said suddenly. "My father did and no one ever asked him for daily women, I dare swear."

"You didn't mind my asking?"

"Dear no — dear no," he said. He had an economical habit of leaving off the first word of a sentence.

His skirts floated as he went wobbling off on his bicycle, looking from the back like a giddy spinster in an old edition of *Punch*, and yet, thought Loveday, he could not be much more than thirty and already dedicated to a life of sacrificial penury. Of course he might become a bishop. Loveday considered this as she cleared away the tea cups and came to the conclusion that it was unlikely.

★ ★ ★

After the doctor's visit Loveday prepared to snatch an hour's sleep. Tom Hove considered that Peter was no worse, but he was puzzled at his reactions to the drug.

"We'll have to put him on to some new stuff if his temperature isn't down by tomorrow," he said.

Loveday suppressed yawns as she watched him go. She so longed for sleep that even her anxiety about Peter was dulled. She felt her eyelids sticking

210

together. Afraid that she might miss five o'clock and the next dose she set the alarm clock, stretched out her legs on the sofa, kicked a cushion on to her toes, which were cold, and she could not face the endless — so it seemed — journey up nine steps to fetch a rug, and was lost in a deep sleep.

She awoke resentfully an hour and a half later to the alarm clock bell and Mrs. Livers tapping on the window.

"I've only just been able to come up, I've had a cold myself," she said breathless, "and being without Mrs. Spracker. That Dolly of hers is a perfect nuisance. The baker told me how bad Peter was. I hadn't worried because he said he had a cold. I'd no idea he was so ill."

Mrs. Livers was not beyond enjoying the drama which illness causes in the country.

"And when I saw a light upstairs, I thought perhaps it was you again. I can't see the caravan from the farm because of the trees, or I might have put two and two together."

Loveday blinked. She never failed to be astonished at the way small pieces of evidence were brought together to make a story with some degree of accuracy. Mrs. Livers sat down and continued:

"I was coming up only I had such a cold myself and then I saw the doctor's car turn in the lane and I knew he couldn't have been anywhere but here, so I thought to myself either Miss Flayne is ill or Peter, so I asked the baker when he came and told me so I came straight away and brought some eggs, the hens are laying well again. I suppose you won't be going to the Institute?"

Mrs. Livers gave the impression of reading a speech from which all punctuation had been deleted.

Loveday explained what had happened.

"Well," said Mrs. livers. "Did you ever? I must say I think it's kind of you to have him. Why ever didn't you come down to us? Though I'm sure I don't know how I'd have managed, only it would have been more suitable."

"Suitable?" echoed Loveday. "With all the work you have to do to saddle yourself with a pneumonia case. It means

212

no sleep for you, you know. It's much better for me to do it."

"Oh, I meant you being single and people talking."

"Talking? What on earth about? I'm old enough to be his mother. If people want to make idiotic suppositions — "

Loveday grew pink with indignation and Mrs. Livers smiled.

"You don't look anything like old enough to be his mother."

"At the moment I feel ninety-nine and I look it," said Loveday defiantly. "What do I do? Flourish my birth certificate?" She began to laugh and she thought when Peter was better this would amuse him.

"People will talk," said Mrs Livers, "you can't stop them — but as long as you don't mind — "

Loveday considered this. She did mind. Then she shook her head. She had a job to do to make Peter well and the tongues of ridiculous busybodies were not going to worry her. She was merely irritable through lack of sleep.

★ ★ ★

During the next few days she had no
cause for feeling lonely. Mrs. Livers
having spread the news at the Women's
Institute and Mr. Livers having done
likewise at the Parish Council meeting
and the Duke's Head, her shopping was
taken over by Mrs. Livers, and a number
of visitors arrived with eggs, illicit butter
and cream, magazines and offers of all
sorts of sick requirements, from brandy
to bed-tables.

Old-fashioned sponge baths were tried,
new-fashioned drugs and by the end
of the fifth day the doctor did not
attempt to hide his alarm. In spite of all
this attention Peter's temperature refused
to fall.

She had help in everything except the
three things she really required. She
wanted most desperately a few hours
uninterrupted sleep and for Peter to
improve. He lay alternately restless,
flinging off his clothes and shouting
incoherently, so that she ran up the
stairs several times in an hour to
make sure he was covered; or he

dozed in a queer coma, seeming to know nothing of where he was or why he was there.

Ann Forstal had called with Roberta. She had been asked to do so by her father, but had had to be nagged into the actual act by Frances, and it was not until K.K. left that she found herself with time again. Frances had told them not to go inside, for she had a horror of germs for Roberta. What Ann breathed she found less serious. The two girls stood, therefore, on the mat and made polite inquiries. Loveday could not conceal her alarm and anxiety, and this Ann passed on to her father when he came home in the evening. He said nothing, but later took the car and said he was going to see Jim Whiteman about the cows on the cricket fields. He did not mention that he intended to call on Loveday on the way over the hill.

★ ★ ★

He parked his car in the gateway to the field to save the tires, and picked his way down the rutted lane towards

Crafers. Loveday had heard no sign of his arrival and he knocked twice before she came to the door. Her eyes were sunk in dark hollows of tiredness and her hair was ruffled in unbecoming disorder. She was expecting Mrs. Livers and when she saw Julian she was filled with dismay. Quickly through her mind leapt the thought that there was nothing to drink in the house but tea, and the fire, which she had lit to defeat this chilly June, was nearly out because she had put off replenishing the log basket from the pile in a dark corner of the yard.

A certain lack of welcome made Julian say: "I won't come in. I just wondered if there was anything I could do for you in Overbridge?"

"Do come in," said Loveday. "The fire is nearly out and it all looks unspeakably sordid."

He fetched logs for her and she blew up the ashes with Miss Cox's bellows. There wasn't even a cigarette in the house for she seldom smoked herself and had forgotten to replenish the box.

"I smoke a pipe anyway," said Julian,

returning with the logs, "if I may?"

"Of course — I'm afraid there isn't a drink either."

"I haven't come to smoke or drink — I've come to see you. Now sit back and relax."

She knew that was what was wrong with her. Normally she let all things blow round her and over her, but now she was taut as a violin string. Her back was rigid, her head ached, she could not read, she could not rest.

"Ann tells me Peter is still pretty ill," said Julian.

"I'm afraid he is."

"We all think it's so kind of you to do this."

"I like looking after people, though I admit I didn't realize he was going to be so ill."

"Isn't he getting better?"

"He lies there so vague about everything. I have been pretty worried, especially not knowing anything about him. Your doctor man has been very kind, but we have wondered each day about trying to find his people, there must be ways and means."

"Perhaps I could look into it for you. Where do I start?"

"Australia House, I suppose. I keep hoping each morning that he will be all right. He does seem a shade better tonight."

"More sensible?"

She laughed. "I wouldn't say that. I mean he's never very sensible. People of his age seldom are. Don't you agree?"

"Don't talk to me of sense. I live in a mad house. Nothing in my house has been the same since Marcy married."

She nodded and looked sympathetic, and he went on to tell her about Ann and Frances and Roberta and Landon.

At half-past nine he was just beginning to tell her about K.K.'s frequent visits.

"There they all sit drinking up my gin and making a hideous row, and I have to restrain myself from hitting them over the head with the tongs."

He sat back looking mildly at her through his glasses, obviously incapable of making his wishes felt with or without the aid of fire-irons.

"I'm very fond of Frances," he continued. "Please don't think I'm not,

218

but I just want some peace. Then, you see, when they've gone I'm even worse off, because then there's no one to look after Johnny. Even if I send him away to school and Ann goes back to her grandmother, there are the holidays."

"And there's still you," said Loveday.

"Me? oh, I see what you mean. Oh, I could rub along. Marcy produces odd bodies who come and go, and I can have my meals at the Duke's Head. That part of it would be rather nice — quiet, you know."

"And you could listen to your own programme on the radio when you wanted to."

"You know the feeling — "

"Yes, but it's selfish and — " she paused, gazing into the fire, her hands clasped round her knees. "It leads to loneliness."

He didn't answer and as they both looked into the fire a moment of silence enveloped them. Then a log fell and Julian leaned forward and pushed it back into the fire. From above they could hear Peter calling.

"I'll have to go up," said Loveday.

"And I must go."

He had forgotten the reason for his call, so pleasant had he found it to sit by the fire and talk to Loveday. He looked round the room seeing nothing but the firelight and the bright backs of the books on the long low shelves. He did not notice the kind of furniture or the colour of the curtains and covers. He only knew that he regretted leaving it.

* * *

When Loveday went up to Peter's bedroom with a hot drink and the inevitable tablets, to her surprise and pleasure she found him lying with his eyes open, and he smiled as if he had been waiting for her.

"My dear boy, I do believe you are better."

She slipped her arm under his shoulders to lift him. He seemed as light and thin as a bird.

"I've stopped aching," he said. "Give it to me, Loveday. I can manage it now."

She sat on the edge of the bed, her heart soft with relief at the unexpected improvement and he took the cup from her and buried his face in it like a small boy.

"Loveday," he said, handing it back. "You are a pet."

"Don't flirt with the nurse," said Loveday, and moved from the bed on to a chair by his side. He turned over and stared at her for a moment with the old scornful look.

"Sorry," he said, turning his head away and closing his eyes. Loveday pulled up the blankets over his shoulders and went softly down the stairs.

11

Convalescence

THE next morning Peter said brightly that he was cured. It was as dramatic as that. His eye was clear and he ate a boiled egg with relish. But when, entirely against Loveday's commands, he put his foot to the ground he fell over and was ignominiously bundled back to bed, looking a little green.

"I am better though," he murmured defiantly, and sat up and demanded the paper.

"You know it never gets up here until after ten. Lie down and go to sleep," said Loveday. Relief made her edgy.

"All right. Don't snap, Loveday dear. It doesn't suit you."

He called out to her cheerfully as she worked round the four rooms. They were never far away from each other, and the doctor came early to hear Loveday carrying on a heated discussion fortissimo as to whether or not dusting was a woman's fetish.

"Ah — better, I hear," Tom Hove said, stepping over the coiled entrails of the vacuum cleaner. Peter was sitting up, washed, shaved and in clean blue pyjamas, looking more than ever like an impertinent boy. He seemed to think he would be allowed up at once, but had to be content with only immediate promotion from the bed-pan and blanket bath to the bathroom.

"He'll be all right now," said Tom Hove. "I thought the stuff would do the trick. Quite dramatic, isn't it, when you think of the old days, but one has to consider that he has been very ill. He mustn't get about too soon. Can you still manage?"

"Oh yes, perfectly easily. It was only not getting any sleep at all that made it a bit difficult, but if he hasn't to have those tablets ever four hours I shall make up for it tonight and I'll be as good as new tomorrow."

"You look tired."

"I am — dead — I'm out of practice, but I'm glad he's better."

"He'll have to think of a holiday — so will you. Queer kid. What does he live on?"

"I've never thought about it. He does casual work for the Livers. I suppose he must have some money."

"Well, sound him about a holiday. No good prescribing something impossible. We'll have to get his chest X-rayed, too. Now that his temperature is down he should be up and about in a week. I'll come again about Thursday."

"When I nursed my mother with pneumonia," mused Loveday, "it was quite different. If these drugs had been available I suppose she might not have died."

"No probably not, and yet I sometimes think that now we keep old people in this world beyond their allotted span."

He lurched out of his chair, lifting up his chin to settle his collar and pulling his pockets. There was always a great deal of unhurried motion about Tom Hove. He reminded Loveday of some large old-fashioned piece of machinery like a mill wheel. He lumbered heavily up the path managing to make sure his stethoscope and notebook were in place, raise his hat and open the gate in one gigantic movement.

Loveday went back into the house, noting the weeds. A pigeon flew with a great stir of wings out of the oak trees. She heard the doctor's brakes screech at the corner of the lane and then there was a moment of stillness and glancing shadows. On the low wall by the kitchen door she sat surverying the bright acres around her, with a feeling of spacious peace, but when she went back into the house she was glad that she was not alone. She heard Peter call:

"Loveday, Loveday. Where are you? Will you bring me some paper and pencil. I could write a bit, I think." There was a querulous edge to his voice.

★ ★ ★

On Wednesday Loveday received a telegram from an old school friend, Janet Salford:

RETURNING FROM GROVE MILL VIA
OVERBRIDGE THIS AFTERNOON HOPE
TO FIND YOU IN.

JANET

It had been handed in two hours earlier at Exeter.

Peter was to be allowed downstairs for lunch, and he was at that moment dressing and singing 'The Flea' in a bass voice of a depth which Loveday found surprising.

"O ho ho ho HO" sang Peter. "A ha ha ha HA." It filled the cottage, and Loveday wondered if Janet would like Peter. She wished there were some means of hiding him. When told of Janet's impending arrival he simply said: "What a bind." There was no tact about him, no shrinking or wondering if he were in the way. He did not even suggest that he should have tea in his bedroom. Gloriously selfish, he asked: "How long do you think she'll stay?"

"Well, I would have asked her for the night, only I can't, with you here," said Loveday tartly, adding in a softer voice, "She probably couldn't have stayed, though. She generally has *plans*."

She smiled a little to herself at the thought of Janet's plans, her journeys dove-tailed to fit in all that she had in mind to do and see. They were miracles of organization, involving lifts from the reluctant husbands of friends, and complicated cross-country rail journeys. They were generally arranged long before and nothing ever went wrong with them, chiefly because Janet was completely ruthless once she had made her plans. You might be dying or your children break their bones, but if you had arranged to meet Janet you made the effort. Good old Janet.

"What's she like?" persisted Peter.

"We were at school together. She's tall. She was quite handsome when she was younger. She is headmistress of a small finishing school."

"Good Lord. She won't show us how to curtsy and what fork to eat with, will she?"

"Don't be crazy. The girls only learn domestic science and typing nowadays. It's really a cheap way of having your house run, I think. Half the chores are done by dukes' daughters, instead of chars, while they learn to housekeep. You'll like Janet, she's good fun, and now I've a lot to do so be a good boy and don't make a mess."

Peter pulled a face and proceeded to sprawl on the sofa and disembowel *The Times*, while Loveday fled into the kitchen, made a cake, renewed the flowers everywhere and brought Peter's room to order. Owing to Mrs. Spracker's absence the brass and silver also needed polishing.

'If I have time,' thought Loveday, working at top speed, and regretting the need to cook Peter's lunch: 'If I have time — '

★ ★ ★

Janet arrived in a new pale-blue Austin car and spent the first ten minutes worrying about the damage she might have done to it by driving up the lane.

"But everyone else does it," protested Loveday, who had forgotten how her friend's possessions always had to be kept in a pristine state.

It was not a successful beginning to the visit and Peter made matters no better by arguing. By the time Loveday returned from switching on the electric kettle something which, in less civilized society, might be described as a brawl was proceeding. In a flash they had both uncovered each other's antagonisms and during the afternoon they ranged acrimoniously over most of the fields in which they were least likely to agree: cars, exhibitions, music, politics and N.A.T.O. Loveday battered her way into the arguments with a calming word, which was scarcely heard. After an hour and a half she noticed that Peter looked tired and she thankfully ordered him to bed. He protested.

"I don't have to go till after supper."

"You go now," said Loveday.

"I'll wash up for you."

"No," Loveday gave a deep sigh. "Look, Peter, stop arguing and go to bed."

He gave a sudden submissive smile only for her, a nod to Janet and disappeared.

He was hardly up the stairs when Janet gave her opinion of him. It was not favourable.

"He isn't always like that. He can be quite charming and he's most intelligent," said Loveday eagerly.

"He has a superficial knowledge of a great many things, and it would be better kept to himself," said Janet.

Loveday privately thought that this statement was justified, but she found she could not bear hearing Peter criticized.

"He has been so ill. Convalescents are always grouchy."

"I think you're very unwise to have him here."

"Unwise? What else could I do?"

"Other means could be found. You're always doing these things and in this case I consider it is particularly silly, because people will talk."

Janet had always prided herself on her broadminded views. She spoke on platforms on divorce law reforms. She was against flogging and capital punishment, and in favour of equal pay for women, but in this small matter of convention her ideas were evidently not far removed from those of Mrs. Livers.

Loveday found that saying she was old enough to be his mother made her feel resentful.

"Janet, dear, don't be so silly. He's just a boy. He might be my son."

"He's in love with you," said Janet severely.

Loveday roared with laughter.

"Of course he isn't. Don't you remember how elderly we found people of forty when we were his age? If folks like to talk about anything so obviously impossible I can't help it. I did what was only neighbourly and next week he'll be back in his caravan, so if you're worrying about my fair name, please stop."

"I'm not worrying," said Janet. "I just hate to think of you making a fool of yourself."

Loveday was not sorry when Janet said she must go as she wanted to get in before it was dark.

The visit had not been a success. Loveday went into the kitchen to wash up the tea things and to get Peter's supper — an unenticing programme.

"What a shocking woman," said Peter cheerfully, when she took up his tray.

"Peter, you were abominable. How could you behave so badly. I was ashamed of you."

"Of me — ashamed of me indeed. She was the rudest thing I've come across in years. Treated me as if I were about five."

"You behaved as if you were about five," said Loveday, pushing her hair out of her eye with a weary gesture.

"I didn't mean to be rude," he said, suddenly meek, "but we just didn't like each other, our auras clashed."

"She's an old friend of mine," pursued Loveday faithfully.

"Are you two the same age?" asked Peter with a note of incredulity in his voice.

Why couldn't she say to Peter: "I am forty-four, Janet if forty-five." Instead she said. "More or less. She's a year older, I think."

"You look ten years younger," said Peter.

"It's only being so small. I'm a great age really." She smiled down at him.

232

"You are just right, dear Loveday," he said.

"Thank you kindly, sir."

Loveday took the tray and manœuvred it down the stairs.

* * *

It was arranged that Peter should return to the caravan the following week. Mrs. Spracker had undertaken to clean it and Loveday had aired the blankets and lit the little stove. She brought in a few flowers and stuck them in a blue jug on the table. The red check curtains and blue covers had been washed by Mrs. Spracker, and it all looked considerably cleaner than it had ever done before.

Loveday looked at his books — Chester Wilmot's *Struggle for Europe*, T. S. Eliot's *Poems*, a well-worn copy of *Rodney Stone*, a dictionary, Bartlett's quotations, Roget's *Thesaurus* and some Penguin thrillers, the *Author's Year Book* and the small impedimenta of a budding writer. Loveday longed suddenly for success for Peter. She had always taken his scribbling lightly, but since she had seen him writing with absorption to a time-table, his food and drink taken only with abstraction, she knew this was to him the most important thing he did, and she wished unaccountably that she could shield him from the inevitable disappointments of such a calling.

★ ★ ★

They had a festive supper together to celebrate Peter's recovery.

"To celebrate my going, you mean," he said gloomily.

They drank each other's health in cider.

"I shall miss you," said Loveday.

"Will you? You've been a darling. Thank you very much, very very much, Loveday."

It was the first time he had voiced his thanks for all she had done. Loveday had privately thought that he took a great deal for granted, but in this she was wrong.

"You've been more than wonderful, Loveday. I — I — I've enjoyed it."

"Dear boy, don't be silly, how could

you? It was a great pleasure to do anything for you."

"Except when I was bloody-minded."

"Exactly so," agreed Loveday.

He carried a load consisting of typewriter, books, and a pair of shoes across the field and returned after a quarter of an hour for the rest of his things. With the house empty for the first time for three weeks, loneliness invaded Loveday. She thought of her dead father and her brother, of Anthony, and of the children she had never borne. It seemed suddenly as if space surrounded her life and kept her away from the love and laughter of others.

Then the latch clicked and Peter came back.

Loveday stood up.

"Do we shake hands," she said.

"No," said Peter calmly. "We kiss," and before she could move he had brushed her cheek lightly.

"Don't flirt with the nurse," said Loveday severely, but the gesture had had a sweet casualness about it which she found unexpectedly moving.

He stood in the doorway slightly

stooping as usual, so as not to knock his head.

"I'm not flirting," he said solemnly. "I love you."

Loveday was startled.

"You can't love anyone as old as I am."

"Why not?"

"It — it's ridiculous, wrong."

"What's wrong about it?"

He held both her hands and she did not answer.

"What's wrong about it? H — m?"

"Well — odd then," she said.

She made to withdraw her hands, but he held them imprisoned.

"And if you think such a thing now — it's just a sick fancy. It will pass," she went on.

"I think not."

He sounded oddly stilted and dropped her hands.

"I've loved you since the minute I set eyes on you, when you wouldn't lend me the bucket."

"That must have been a romantic moment," mocked Loveday.

She gave him a teasing smile.

"Don't you like me at all?" he asked.

"Of course I do, you funny boy; of course I like you."

"Oh well," he said. She knew that he would say as he always did, 'one of those things', and she was right. He was half out of the door when he turned suddenly and added: "I know you think I'm young and silly, but I'm not either. I've been in love before."

"And you will be again," said Loveday gently.

"I daresay, that's not the point."

She could see him bracing up for an argument. He suddenly looked tired and white. She put her hand on his arm and turned him gently towards the door. At the door he said roughly:

"I haven't said this before, Loveday, because of — well — being a guest — of a sort — and you being on your own here."

She was touched by his chivalry.

"But I tell you I absolutely adore you. I've never met anyone quite like you before and I — I — can't get you out of my mind."

To her amazement she perceived as

the light caught his face that his eyes were full of tears.

"You've got to love me a bit, Loveday, you've got to."

Loveday was moved by unaccountable emotions, all the more disturbing because they were so unexpected. She put her arm up to his shoulder with a gesture she might have used to comfort an unhappy child, and was suddenly held close to him and kissed with fierce intensity and then he was gone. She had not even time to protest.

As she returned to the empty room she realized she hadn't wanted to protest.

12

Taking The Waters

SHE had spent most of the night wondering what would be the right, even the proper, thing to do after Peter's sentimental outburst of the day before. That he fancied himself in love with her she found touching, and she could not decide what would be the wisest and kindest course to take. No one had fallen in love with her for a long time, and she had consoled herself for a certain emptiness in her life by the thought that it was at least peaceful. She did not want to be disturbed again. At forty-four she might consider herself middle-aged, she told herself, although the words made the state unenticing but she also had no mind to be made to appear ridiculous, and she determined to deal hardly with Peter.

She made up her mind that she would go out for the day. For some time she had been wanting to go to Avonbury Spa to see an old cousin of her father's and to buy a summer dress and at six o'clock, after hours of wakefulness, she determined to go there on the early train.

Avonbury Spa was far enough away to make the journey a reason for a day's outing, even with a car. By bus and train it was even more complicated and would take, Loveday realized, about two and a half hours.

It was a fine clear morning and the weather forecast was announced cheerfully by the announcer to fit. After consulting the time-table she decided to walk to the village and catch the eight o'clock bus to Overbridge, going on from there by train. From across the field the caravan gave no sign of life.

She selected a thin grey suit from her wardrobe which she had not worn since she left London. Avonbury, she had heard, had a reputation for fashion. She would wear a hat. This presented difficulties, for she now seldom wore a hat and she felt suddenly dressed up and out of place, but she decided on her

240

grey felt trimmed with pale blue cords to match a linen blouse, and she was artlessly pleased with the effect.

Until she was in the train at Overbridge she felt over-dressed amongst the shapeless tweeds, jerseys and washed-out cotton frocks of Overbridge, but once in Avonbury she had that feeling, so pleasing to any woman, that she was well and suitably clad. She stepped forth with a spring in her step.

The town, made famous in the days of the Georges, straggled up and down a hill. At the bottom, steps led into a small cobbled square which was barred to traffic, and here, under the colannades where Beau Brummel had once strolled and drunk the waters (still spouting forth from a dingy spring at the corner at a penny a glass) a certain air of leisure remained. At eleven and three o'clock the band of the Halberdiers played the *William Tell* Overture and stirring tunes from *The Mikado* to a shifting audience lolling under the lime trees.

It was half-past ten when she arrived, and after a brief look round and a cup of coffee she set out to find the Regent Hotel where her father's cousin was staying. It was a little walk beyond the square over a small common, and here she found her, miserable with rheumatism, but otherwise comfortable at, as she pointed out to Loveday, considerable expense. Loveday listened patiently to a recital of the drawbacks of living at the Regent, the incivility of a chambermaid, now sacked, the iniquity of the boots, who would whistle, the endless tittle-tattle of the other guests, who crept about the lounge in various stages of decrepitude.

The younger woman found it all unbearably depressing and she thought suddenly of her own old age, lonely and loveless. The picture of it stood between her and the sun as she took her leave and wondered what she should do next.

She walked slowly up the hill pausing at every antique shop and searching unsuccessfully in the small dress shops for what she had in mind. By the time she reached the upper end of the town, the road crossing by the old Opera House, now a cinema, had completely changed character, and all the eighteenth-century leisure of the Pump Square was left behind. Buses roared past the red and gold splendours of Woolworth's and Marks and Spencer's. Dresses crowded each other in stores, instead of being displayed in costly solitude; cakes, with no pretence at being home-made, were whipped into paper bags by pert girls. There were no more antique shops and only one book-shop. It was not so much Avonbury Spa as anywhere in England where progress has laid its hand.

Loveday had, as yet, bought nothing, but she was happy and optimistic as she walked up one side of the street and down the other in bright sunlight. It was not until after lunch that she had a curious feeling of lacking a companion. At the café where she chose her lunch the tables were full of couples ranging from middle-aged women exchanging confidences to quiet lovers gazing at each other in corners. At the end of the restaurant a group of tables had been set aside for a Women's Institute outing, and soon they arrived, noisy with the excitement of a day away from home. Loveday picked up a magazine, averted her eyes from the resentful couple who had been forced to share her table and ordered a meagre lunch.

It was at this point that she stopped enjoying herself. There was no train until four thirty-seven, and the comfort of her own home seemed far away. She thought of Peter, idiotic boy that he was, with a certain affection and then pushed him resolutely to the back of her mind. From the Pump Square came the sounds of the band, and she walked down the hill towards it and paid for a chair. The sun flickered through the leaves of lime trees; people talked unconcernedly, children ran about among the chairs, but Captain Ferrers of the Halberdiers, slim in a black uniform trimmed with gold braid, waved an elegant baton, fluttering his left hand, turning his head this way and that to bring the Halberdiers to their final crescendo. There was a pause, a rustle of papers, and a general shifting. A man from the Avonbury Spa Corporation demanded sixpence. Behind Loveday a boy picked up a girl: "Go to the pictures much?" he asked. "Depends who with," giggled the girl.

Captain Ferrers announced that Lance-Corporal Smith of the Halberdiers would now sing 'Glorious Devon'. It was ridiculous, thought Loveday, how oddly stirring it was, even when the Lance-Corporal Smith did not quite hit the note.

The clapping sounded flat in the open air. Loveday rose and walked slowly down the colonnade, contemplating tea. Her eye was caught by some small prints in a shop at the corner, of Avonbury in the pre-Woolworth era, an illustration from an old guide book perhaps, amateurishly splodged with colour. She stepped forward to peer more closely and then back to consider whether it was worth fifteen shillings. In doing this she knocked clumsily against a passer-by.

"I beg your pardon."

A hat was raised. A look of incredulous pleasure came over the man's face. It was Julian Lenham.

"I've been seeing over a school for Johnny. You see, I took your advice."

"I didn't know I gave any," smiled Loveday. "I hope the school was nice, suitable, I mean."

"Tom Hove's boy goes there and seems to like it."

"And you?"

"Oh, I suppose it was all right. I didn't know what to look for. When I went to school it was taken for granted that you were miserable and underfed and slept cheek by jowl and lived in a perpetual draught. This place was centrally heated and they insisted on showing me the kitchens."

"But of course. Were they good?"

"How should I know? They were large and clean and full of enormous shepherd's pies, made with real shepherds, I don't doubt. When I asked if the boys learnt anything the head-master seemed quite surprised. Look, are you having tea or something?"

"Just about to."

"May we have it together. Where shall we go? That place on the corner looks as if it might do. After two hours of that I feel as if I've forgotten to put my gym shoes away and may get fifty lines at any moment."

Loveday laughed. She sat eating buttered toast and listening to Julian's continued account of his day.

"Now tell me what you've been doing," he said, and she told him about the cousin, the Women's Institute outing and Glorious Devon. She had had a lovely day, she said, the sun had shone, Avonbury was delightful, she didn't wonder that the Prince Regent had liked it. The loneliness was all forgotten.

"Good heavens, my train goes at four thirty-seven."

"I've got the car. I can give you a lift back if you don't mind waiting for me. I have to see a client at five o'clock. It will only take half an hour or so and then I can drive you back. It's a pretty run, over Black Hill, and you won't be much later home than if you took the train. The service is abominable. Don't tell me you came by train."

"How else?" said Loveday. "But it doesn't matter what time I get home. I have only myself to please."

Her freedom had a bleak sound.

"How's that young man?"

"Back in his caravan."

She had an impulse to tell him about

Peter. She could make a good story of it. But somehow she could not. It was no longer funny either to her or to Peter, so she changed the subject.

★ ★ ★

He did not arrive at the door of the Grand Pump Hotel, where they had arranged to meet, until nearly six, apologizing for the delay. Loveday had left him an hour before with such a feeling of exhilaration that all things had become possible. In half an hour she found and bought exactly the right dress, a pair of shoes, two books and the print of Avonbury Spa, and she now sat in a leather chair of the Grand Pump looking out on to the emptying square. The shops in the colonnade were closed. The old woman at the corner by the Spring was polishing the glasses while her daughter counted the takings. The band of the Halberdiers were all in the Leopards' Head, fortifying themselves for the evening performance with beer.

It was the pleasant end of a pleasant day, thought Loveday, as Julian brought her a dry Martini.

"I'm sorry about the parcels," she said, after refusing a second cocktail. He took the two largest and said he didn't mind a bit. Dangling a ridiculous string on one finger he thought that he hadn't been hung with feminine parcels since the first years of his marriage, and then there had always been an argument. The quick acrimony of Judy suddenly came alive. She would argue about the cost, the size, the shape, and who should carry them, and unless he kept absolutely silent the discussion became a disagreement, the disagreement a brawl. He had learnt to speak his mind seldom, if ever.

As they crossed the square to the car park Loveday wondered at his silence, but she was not a woman who liked perpetual talk and she walked beside him without speaking.

"I was thinking," he said at last, as he packed her parcels into the back of the car, "that it's a long time since I did anything so domestic as female shopping."

Loveday wondered about his wife. All she knew of her was gossip. She had been killed in an air raid. She had been beautiful and amusing, a devastating combination. It was not surprising that he had not married again.

"Don't you shop for Ann or Mrs. Lowesmore or your sister?"

"Heaven forbid! Anyway, Ann buys everything in London in great comfort with her grandmother's chauffeur to drive her, and Frances wouldn't trust me," he paused. "Odd relationship, brother and sister. Frances seems most of the time to have turned into a foreigner and I have a hell of a job liking Landon, and as for Roberta, I could slap her, but every now and then Frances and I remember things that belong to no one else."

"And a wall grows round you both," said Loveday softly.

"You know — exactly — you know."

"I have a brother myself."

"Tell me," he said gently and she found as they drove towards Black Hill under an arch of trees that she could indeed talk of him of many things, of Alan, of Miss Cox of Crafers, of the years of her parents. But of Anthony Flexford she said little, of Peter she said nothing.

They came down into Foxhurst and up its straggling street where the road forked for Overbridge. On the corner was the Bay Leaf, its car park full, its window-boxes ablaze. Julian pulled up.

"Shall we stop for some dinner here?" he asked. "Or must you go home?"

"No — must you?"

"Alas no. Frances has taken the family over to Marcy's for the day and I am being left something cold out of a tin." He pulled a face. "Let's dine here. It has a new manager and is supposed to be good."

She thanked him and said: "I should enjoy it very much."

The bar was small and not completely spoiled by the renovations of the new management. A plethora of pewter mugs and horse brasses failed to conceal completely the charm of a room which was low-beamed and friendly, with chintz-covered chairs and a large bowl of flowers.

They had not booked a table and the restaurant was full. The manager came forward respectfully doubtful as to whether there was room for them.

"We can wait," said Julian, adding as he turned to Loveday, "unless of course you're in a particular hurry?"

"No," said Loveday.

The days were her own, the nights were her own, her life stretched before her, uncluttered and free. Somehow she wished it were not so.

There was, reflected Loveday, as she repaired her face in the ladies' cloakroom, something unhurried about Julian Lenham. When she returned he was standing by the window and she saw his thin, unathletic silhouette against the light. His clothes hung badly, partly because he filled every pocket, so that his coat sagged and drooped as if the seams were lead weighted. His sandy hair, however short he kept it, was perpetually ruffled. His glasses gave him a studious look, which was belied by the apparent fury of his gaze, due, though Loveday did not know this, to the near-blindness of his right eye, caused by a war wound. This made him wheel round when he spoke and stare with an earnestness which many found disconcerting. After Peter's moods and conversation it was

252

refreshing to be back in one's own generation where one belonged. She appreciated the certainty with which Julian did most things, from ordering *homard à l'Américaine* and a nineteen forty-nine *Liebfraumilch*, to tipping the waiter with obvious adequacy.

He told her about the Roman Villa at Rotheringham; how the stones for Overbridge Church had been quarried under Black Hill and ferried by water down the Frayle river, now a sluggish brook choked with weeds, and how some of the stones, after the church was damaged by fire, had been used in the Friar's House.

"It's our coal-hole now," he added. "There's an Early English arch which you can see quite plainly. We had the Archæological Society from Hinwood over and they poked about amongst the coke and decided it must be part of the monk's cellar."

★ ★ ★

By the time they set off for the journey home the view from Black Hill was hidden in darkness.

"We must come another time in the light," said Julian. "It really is rather a sight. Your cottage is at one end of the ridge and Black Hill at the other and from here you can see away over the moors to the sea."

"Wider horizon," said Loveday, seeing Crafers in her mind's eye perched on its hill top with its own view.

"Yes, altogether wider."

He saw immediately that Loveday meant more than the actual words she said. It was a relief that one had so little explaining to do to Julian. His memory stretched back over the same period of years. She already thought of him as Julian, though she did not call him by his Christian name. They both came of an era when using a Christian name was a stage of intimacy like *tutoyer* in France, or the impressive moment in Germany when one drank *Brüderschaft*, so that she was surprised when he said as he changed down for the steep descent into the valley:

"I expect you know my name is Julian. But I don't know what yours is."

"It's Loveday, it's queer, I used to hate it. It's a family name."

She was always embarrassed about her name. It either roused shouts of laughter or rather precious praise: 'My dear, how touching, how altogether pot-pourri and brass-bed.'

Julian only repeated: "Loveday, I like it. It suits you."

The stars were shining by the time they reached Crafers. They now knew as much about each other as they had chosen to tell. The picture that each had of the other was impressionist rather than photographic, but it served to make them both feel as if they had become friends.

Julian left his car at the corner of the lane to avoid the awkward turn at the end in the dark and walked with her to the gate carrying her parcels. She wondered if she should ask him in for a drink, and decided against it. He was probably sick of the sight of her after five hours.

Holding out her hand she said: "Thank you very much," giving a slight emphasis to the polite words which overlaid them with sincerity.

"Thank you," he said, shaking her hand firmly, and glaring with friendly ferocity, as he handed over the parcels.

The moon shone enough to illumine the squat outline of Crafers and the straight path to her front door. There was a faint glow about it, which puzzled her, and when she opened the door she discovered that it was a light shining from the kitchen. She stopped suddenly, her heart tight, her mind rushing from the peaceful country of friendship and laughter into a fearful depth of cosh-armed burglars. It was at such moments that she longed for a telephone.

Julian was by now half-way down the lane.

"Who's there?" she called.

There was no answer. She dropped her parcels and gingerly opened the door.

In Miss Cox's old chair by the side of the fireplace was Peter, only now waking from a deep sleep. For the moment he seemed as astonished to see Loveday as she was to see him.

"What are you doing here? You gave me a horrible fright," she said, furious with relief.

He ignored her question and shot one of his own at her.

"Where have you been?"

"I have been to Avonbury and it's nothing to do with you at all where I go and what I do. What I want to know is, how you got in."

"Through the door. It was open, and even if it hadn't been I know where you keep the key."

He looked at her defiantly.

She thought back. In the swiftness of her decision to get away she had forgotten to lock the door.

"You have no business to walk in and out of my house like this, and scare the wits out of me!"

Only now she realized how frightened she had been. She sat in the chair he had vacated and felt suddenly a little sick.

"Loveday, dear Loveday, I didn't mean it like that at all. I've been here so much. I — I never thought you'd mind and I was worried about you, honestly I was. Were you really scared? Shall we have some tea?"

She nodded, and he filled the kettle and went with familiar ease to the cupboard to get out his own big cup, a bath of a cup with roses on it, which he had found in Miss Cox's china cabinet and appropriated during his stay, and a smaller one for Loveday. She watched him fetch sugar and milk.

"I couldn't think what had happened to you," he said. "I came over in the morning to — to apologize."

She had nearly forgotten in the pleasures of the day and her fright at seeing him any incident which might demand an apology. Now she remembered, and she heard his voice going on:

"You were out, so I watched for your coming back and you didn't, and then, when it was dark, I did begin to worry."

She saw his too long hair flop forward as he bent over the tea-tray and she suppressed a jerk of amusement that he should suppose anything he said or did should make her throw herself under a train, as he obviously feared.

"Loveday, are you all right?"

"Perfectly, thank you. The kettle's boiling, put in plenty of tea."

She kept the uneasy conversation down

to the level of the tea cups.

"I just thought it was a lovely day and I'd never been to Avonbury."

"Why didn't you tell me? I could have taken you in the car. It's a lousy journey by train."

"It wasn't. I enjoyed it and I ran into Julian Lenham and he brought me home, and we had dinner on the way at Foxhurst. That's why I'm late."

He put the cups down noisily.

"The hell you are," he said. She realized that for some reason he was blazing with anger.

"Do you like the fellow?" he asked, biting the words.

Loveday looked at him mildly.

"I've never thought about it. He's kind and has good manners. He knows a lot about archæology. You'd have been interested."

"I doubt it."

"Your tea is getting cold."

After the peaceful relaxation of the day Loveday could feel her thoughts tightening inside her head. She had made a great effort to swing the conversation to impersonal things. Had the baker left her a loaf and did Peter think it was going to rain the next day?

"Not according to the wireless," said Peter more calmly. "That's really what I wanted to talk to you about. I thought perhaps you'd let me take you to the sea if it's fine."

She did not want to go to the sea. She wanted to catch up with her housework and gardening.

"Do, please, Loveday. I do miss you so," he added, "and I'm due for a day out before I start again at the farm."

"You ought to go away for a holiday."

"So old Hove says, but I don't know where to go. I can't afford it really, and anyway I don't want to go."

His voice had the peevishness of a small child.

Loveday still hesitated. Dislike of the idea made her ungracious.

"Oh well," he said, "if you don't want to, it doesn't matter."

He lurched himself out of his chair so that the back creaked.

"Anything you want me to do before I go?" he asked, his jealous hurt changing the tone of his voice and the intonation of his words so that ice was in them.

"Look, Peter," said Loveday on an impulse. "I don't want to be unkind, but I really have a lot of things to do tomorrow and Mrs. Spracker comes."

"I can help you. What have you got to do?"

"Masses of odd jobs and you couldn't help me."

"If it's fine the next day will you come?"

Loveday sighed and gave up with a laugh.

"All right — if it's fine."

"It had better be," he said joyously, suddenly happy and alive again. "Bless you, my darling, but I do love you."

He blew her a kiss and was gone.

13

The Golden Margin

IT was one of the few hot days in that wet summer. The flaming sunset, the weather forecast and Mrs. Spracker's corns all boded well for the outing to the sea and the evening before, as dusk fell, Loveday straightened her back and put away her fork and hoe. The soft air in the garden and the total absence of Peter had given the day a beneficent quality. Not even the sound of his gramophone or wireless disturbed the stillness.

A knock on the front door after dark was a rare thing and she called out to know who was there.

"Only me," said Peter's voice.

She undid the bolts.

It was a long time since he had even knocked at the back door and he had certainly never used the front one before. It opened directly into the sitting-room and he stood politely on the mat, unfamiliar in a dark grey suit and white shirt, waiting to be asked in.

"Good heavens. I couldn't imagine who it could be."

"Well, I thought perhaps I'd been a bit too free with the key and the door. Surely you can't mind my knocking on the front door like a respectable caller?"

"At ten o'clock at night?"

"Loveday dear, don't be difficult. I won't come in."

"You may if you like."

"No, I just wanted to know about times for tomorrow. Eleven-ish?"

He stood on the mat as if a barrier lay before him.

Loveday agreed, and asked if she should bring a picnic lunch.

"I've got it all laid on," he said. "I went to Hinwood today and I've brought ham and rolls and a tin of pineapple. You do like pineapple, don't you?" he added anxiously.

"Adore it."

"You could make some coffee if you like. My thermos always tastes of thermos."

He looked so young and eager in his

unexpectedly tidy clothes with his hair brushed and tie neatly tied. Loveday had never seen him before in anything but jerseys and corduroys and she did not realize that his shoulders were so square and straight.

"You look incredibly smart," she said. "You put me to shame."

"I've been all day in Hinwood and got them to look at the car and make sure it is all right and went to the bank and had my hair cut. You said you liked it short."

The sight of his well-shaped head shorn to an unfamiliar smoothness touched her.

"And bought the ham?"

"Yes. It's going to be fine."

He was jubilant and after he had gone, whistling across the field, Loveday was touched by the thoughts of all his preparations. Up to that moment she had been half hoping it would rain, but now she could not bear the thought of disappointment for him.

His preparations did not end there. The next day, before Loveday was up, he was cleaning the red car, polishing the little stream-lined goddess which adorned the bonnet, padding the broken spring with cushions. At eleven he appeared and sounded the horn. It was the only new thing on the car and it split the silence, brought Loveday running from the house in the new brown and white striped dress she had bought at Avonbury, a jersey over her arm. When she saw that the ramshackle hood was down she stopped.

"I thought it would be pleasanter to have it down," said Peter. "It's going to be hot, but I'll put it up again if you mind."

Loveday had not travelled in an open car since she was in her twenties. There came a moment when she prepared to be less windswept. However, all she said was:

"How nice," adding, "perhaps I'd better run back for my scarf or my hair will blow to pieces."

"And a thicker coat," called Peter.

It seemed ridiculous on such a hot day to be going back into the house for a big coat and scarf. 'If I'd known', thought Loveday irritably, 'I would have dressed quite differently,' though she was vain enough to realize that the brown and white cotton dress suited her well, and when she was eventually stowed into the car, muffled against the wind rushing past her ears and blowing back her eyelashes, she had to admit it was an exhilarating sensation.

She had forgotten how much more there was to be seen from an open car, the limitless vault of pale-blue sky stretching across beyond the moorland to the sea. For a few miles they travelled along the road to Foxhurst, which she had seen for the first time only the day before yesterday, and now there was a width and breathlessness about it which made it seem almost a different country. She found herself anticipating the day with excited enjoyment.

Owing to the age of the car's tyres a puncture was almost inevitable, but as this happened shortly after noon, close by the Katerstone, on the top of the moors before the road dropped to the sea, it turned out to be a pleasant interlude. Loveday shed her scarf, spread her coat on the springy turf and leant back against the Katerstone and lit a cigarette. She wondered about its history and thought that when she next saw Julain she would ask him. On the road below her Peter wrestled with wheels, wiped his oily hands on a clean handkerchief and then suggested lunch.

"Or shall we wait until we get down to the beach?"

"No — here," said Loveday, "it's the perfect place."

He brought up the two baskets and they moved round to the shadow of the stone, for the sun was high. Peter sat down on the other half of her coat. Bees buzzed in the heather and somewhere out of sight droned an aeroplane. A dazzle of light lay over the distant sea. Loveday was not in the least hungry but Peter played such an anxious host that she ate ham rolls and pineapple washed down with cider and her own coffee, and then thought uneasily of indigestion.

"I'm always hungry," said Peter.

"You don't cook proper meals," accused Loveday.

"I used to," said Peter, "but staying with you spoilt me a bit and now I can't be bothered."

"But you must eat sensibly or you'll never get well."

"I am well," said Peter truculently, "I start work on Monday.

Indeed he was marvellously recovered from his illness, except for a certain thinness.

"I wrote to Mother and told her how wonderful you'd been. I expect she'll write to you. I wonder if you'd like my mother."

"I expect I should. Are you like her?"

"No," he said shortly. "People say she's very pretty. My step-sister is like her but I've only seen her once. She's only six."

He had never mentioned his step-father and from this Loveday surmised a dislike, but she was an incurious person and was only interested in what people chose to tell her. Perhaps for this reason she was often told a great deal.

"He's a wart, you know, my step-father, awful type."

"Is he? I expect you're a bit jealous."

"Yes, I expect I am, but he's a wart."

He threw a stone viciously across the heather and it rolled away down the hill and they heard its gentle knocking after it was out of sight.

"Don't do that, you'll hurt someone on the road," said Loveday.

"Sometimes I feel I'd like to hurt someone."

"Cosh boy," teased Loveday.

He chewed a grass pensively. "None of the people I love love me," he said suddenly.

"The world is a full place and one day someone will."

"They never do — even my mother."

"You're very possessive, you know. It's an unhappy thing to be. You can't expect your mother not to marry again."

"But such a wart," he repeated.

"For a writer your powers of description appear to be limited. My dear, accept him — as a wart if you must — but accept him."

"I can't. I want everything to be mine. Like the way I want you," he added softly.

Loveday sat back against the rigid Katerstone and was filled with pity and dismay. She ought never, she thought, to have come on this expedition. It was simply teasing the boy. She had never considered that his feeling for her was anything more than a quick flash of affection born of loneliness and propinquity. Now, with misgiving she began to wonder. She looked across the moor without speaking. He threw away the grass and began leisurely to chew another.

"Aren't we going to the sea," she said, jumping up and tying on her scarf.

He helped her on with her coat and in silence they collected the lunch remains.

The road dropped steeply towards the coast. Ahead of them glinted the sea edged with a ribbon of sand.

"The golden margin," said Peter as they watched it grow nearer until they could park the car on a low cliff and scramble down to the beach.

'At least,' thought Loveday, struggling modestly into her bathing suit behind an inadequate rock, 'I'm not fat,' but she felt suddenly self-conscious, revealed in the elegant remains of the year before last's holiday in the South of France, and she plunged quickly into the shelter of the water.

She had swum slowly across the bay to a rock before she saw Peter run across the sands looking like part of a Greek frieze. He swam effortlessly like a fish, having learnt in the warm seas on Bondi Beach as soon as he could walk, and she saw him heading out to sea and watching his head bobbing on the water, so far away that when he turned she sighed with relief.

He did not join her on the rock but lay on the sand nearby, puffing and exhausted.

"Idiot," she said, "you aren't fit enough to swim so far. And it's still horribly cold."

He grinned without answering.

"Showing off," went on Loveday.

"Lord, girl. How you nag."

Loveday clambered off the rock and made her way to her clothes and handbag for chocolate and cigarettes. A ridiculous exhilaration filled her that he had called her a 'girl'. She looked back at him as he lay spread-eagled on the sand, his shoulders still heaving with his deep breaths.

'One could be very fond of him,' she thought.

In preparation for a lazy day on the beach she had brought her knitting and a book, but as soon as she was dressed Peter called across from his rock and suggested a walk. They scrambled up a gully on to the cliff top and set off along a grassy path towards the lighthouse.

It looked deceptively near, but it must have been two miles away and when they at last reached it Loveday discovered that she was expected to climb to the top. Unprotesting, she counted the steps, two hundred and fifty, and when she was at the top a bad head for heights took away any enjoyment. But Peter walked round the platform gay and cheerful, talking to the lighthouse keeper. Loveday discovered at the end of the expedition, when they had walked back to the car, that she was tired and wanted nothing so much as a cup of tea. She had no sooner mentioned this than she found herself being driven to Felsbourne, a busy resort five miles to the east.

Felsbourne began with disused tram-lines and a gasworks surrounded by early twentieth-century red-brick villas. As they came nearer to the town, pin-table saloon, ice-cram parlours, fish and chip bars took their place. Beyond the pier Loveday could see the Regency houses and the better hotels. A small harbour, still picturesque because nothing the council could devise could utterly destroy the charm of the places which are full of boats and sailors, separated the two ends of the town. There was a powerful smell of fish.

Peter parked the car and led the way to a small café where a cheerful blonde was standing behind an urn. He brought Loveday some tea, forgetting that she disliked sugar, but she drank it gratefully and revived in time for Peter to take her on the pier. She was weighed, she had her fortune told and an artist made a surprisingly good silhouette of her. She ate an ice-cream sandwich and refused to ride in a speed boat.

"I hate them," she said. "I'm always sick. You go."

She sank gratefully into a deck chair and watched him whirred across the bay waving his handkerchief. She thought:

'I shall be dead tomorrow,' but at the moment she was seized by Peter's mood and when he came back and suggested that they went to the Felsbourne Follies after they had had something to eat she gaily agreed.

"You oughtn't to be tearing about like this. Come and sit down."

He came and sat by the side of her for half an hour and for the first time they relaxed and did nothing, and Loveday thought of her knitting. Separated by a merciful amount of distance, Felsbourne looked like a French town, the sails in the harbour decorating the view like gay ribbon bows. The empty deck chairs at their side made forlorn flaps in the breeze as the pier gradually emptied.

"Your nose has grown freckles," said Peter, examining Loveday solemnly. "I can see them popping out."

"I was a horrible sight as a child — covered in them," said Loveday.

"I wish I'd known you then."

Loveday laughed. "You weren't even thought of," she said.

"Funny, isn't it?" he went on, clasping one knee and looking back at the shore.

"You're so much older, and yet I love you so desperately. I've never felt like this about anyone before."

"People in love always say that. It is different each time."

"Yes, I suppose it is, but I have a feeling I'll never forget you, that when I'm an old, old man I shall think of you."

"By that time I shall have been dead for years. My dear, there's a gap between us which one can't cross."

"I can," he said defiantly. Then he jumped up. "I'm sorry, I made a solemn resolve that I wouldn't worry you today. I just want you to be happy. Are you?"

"Yes," said Loveday truthfully. "I'm enjoying it very much. Go and get me an evening paper, there's a lamb."

He walked off, his hands in pockets, and she watched his back, jaunty, confident. Then, as his figure gradually diminished and turned into a midget, but still recognizable as Peter, going through the turnstile, a queer sensation shot through her heart. It was like nothing which had ever assailed her emotions or senses before. She felt as if everything

275

were lighter about her, as if something warm and glowing had taken possession of her.

'Good heavens,' she thought aghast, feeling quickly for her knitting, 'if I'm not careful I shall think myself in love.' She heard Janet's warning voice. 'I don't want you to look ridiculous.'

But she didn't feel ridiculous. She only felt as if living were a more delightful prospect than ever. She put down her knitting and watched for Peter's return.

When he came back with an assortment of papers she thought he looked tired, but he hotly denied it, though he consented to sit down for a while longer, and they read the papers in companionable silence. It was still warm, though the sun began to sink behind the moors.

"If we go to the Follies," said Peter, "I can't take you out to dinner. They start at seven. I got the tickets when I went for the papers, second row of the stalls. No expense spared. I expect it will be frightful," he added gloomily.

"No, it won't, and anyway I'm in the mood to enjoy anything, and we can eat afterwards. I'm not a bit hungry."

"Try this."

From his pocket he produced a stick of rock.

"Felsbourne all the way through," he said.

"Thank you," said Loveday. "I adore rock. It makes me feel about five. We used to come to places like this when we were children and my father always bought me rock. They were quite pleasant then, you know, without amusement arcades and ice-cream stalls. If a place had donkeys and a pier we thought it was awfully sophisticated."

She saw her childhood as a relic of another simpler age. She was thirteen before her father bought a car. She could clearly remember the first time she saw an aeroplane, and heard the new miracle of radio. It was a world as far removed from Peter as the stern Victorianism her mother had so often described.

"Shall we go and have a drink?" asked Peter.

Loveday shuddered at the thought of the taste of anything on the top of Felsbourne rock. She chewed manfully and departed in the direction of a door marked 'Ladies' which she penetrated through an iron turnstile. Two girls were discussing pin-up perms and fussing with each other's hair. Their faces were round and youthful and they examined their features with ill-concealed admiration. Grudgingly they ceded Loveday the corner of the mirror, from which she dusted powder over new freckles and refurbished her lipstick. Her hair, when combed, fell back neatly into its soft waves.

An inadequate wash did little to remove the feeling that even the new dress had lost its freshness. The two girls shook powder over the floor and basin and departed, meeting their escorts outside with loud cries.

The Follies were better than Loveday expected, even when seen from the second row of the stalls and, if she felt occasionally embarrassed at the lowness of the humour, she was probably unique. In the interval she listened enthralled to other people's conversations. 'She did ought to wear corsets,' said a voice behind her, and another voice agreed that 'it didn't do to let yer figger go'.

She caught Peter's eye and was glad for someone to share the joke, realizing how often there was no one to do this. Again she felt an odd surge of affection for him. His elbow touched hers on the hard wooden arm between them; chocolate papers rustled behind as the corsetless one was further discussed.

On the stage a pretty girl poised uncertainly on her toes and an elderly tenor sang 'One enchanted evening'.

There really was, thought Loveday, as they came out into the warm dark, an enchantment about it all, about Peter's masterful hand on her arm, the walk along the front, the lights swinging across the darkness by courtesy of the ratepayers from June to September, the excellence of the egg and chips in a harbour café, the beer at the Ship Inn. What was there about it to give it a magic quality? Any single item offered to Loveday at any other time for her entertainment would have been refused, and yet here she was sitting with Peter on a bench outside a frowsty bar watching the harbour lights, the gently lapping water, and listening to the juke-box imported for the benefit of the American airmen from Menning Camp, as if pleasantly bewitched.

★ ★ ★

Their car stood alone in the middle of the deserted car park. It was as if they had waited until every bit of pleasure had been squeezed out of Felsbourne. The lights went out.

"Will you be cold if I leave it open," said Peter.

Loveday privately thought that she would, but she shook her head and allowed herself to be helped into the coat and scarf.

"It's late," she said.

"We'll go down the big coast road. We'll be home in an hour," said Peter. "Gosh! I've loved today. I don't want it to end."

He said this so simply that Loveday was moved with something between love and pity. She gave one of those half-smiles of hers, which, had she known it, lit her face with great charm.

"Good heavens, Loveday," said Peter bluntly, tucking rugs round her and

280

giving the contents of the car a brief stir in order to make room for her. "Why on earth didn't you ever marry?"

It was so long since she had considered the question that she wondered how to answer.

"There was only one person I ever really wanted to marry, apart from being in love, I mean," she said slowly.

"Why didn't you marry him?"

"He had a wife," said Loveday dully.

"Oh, couldn't you do anything about it?"

"Not really. She was a friend of mine anyway and that made it more difficult. He spoilt me for other people. And he didn't really love me enough."

She saw clearly now that this was so. Peter started the car and the wind whipped her face. She had always done the loving, she thought. That was why she was sorry for Peter.

It was at that moment that she resolved to go away. She saw herself closing the house, packing her clothes, telephoning the President of the Women's Institute, writing to Mrs. Spracker. It was ridiculous how complicated it was to leave one tiny perch, but she must do it, she saw clearly, not only for Peter's sake, but for her own. Her cheeks chilled in the wind as she wondered where she should go.

At the end of the wide coastal road they turned up the lane through Brinscome Woods, which led to the old Overbridge turnpike. The moon was hidden, rabbits ran distractedly across the path of their lights; the cold air sang in their ears. Suddenly Peter pulled up.

Loveday looked at him in dismay.

"Don't give me that scared look, darling. I won't touch you," he said, belying his words by taking her hand.

And then to Loveday's horror she saw his shoulders shake and she knew that he was crying.

She had seen men cry before and she well knew that tears were not a woman's privilege, but they always horrified her. She put her arm round him and felt his tears wet on her cheek.

"Peter, dear boy, don't," she said.

He stayed motionless in her arms and

she made small comforting noises as if he were a hurt, small boy, and then suddenly he was no longer in her arms, she was in his. She had forgotten the impatience of young love.

14

Flight

LOVEDAY was in London. The room which Alan had said would always be there for her was her obvious refuge. She sent a telegram and packed before she could change her mind. She was not running away for Peter's sake but for her own. Ridiculous though it might be, she knew now that she was in love with Peter, just as he was in love with her, and although at first everything had suddenly seemed brightened, colours sharper, words with more meaning, although perhaps some brief idiotic happiness might come of it, she knew it was doomed. It was wrong — and it was laughable, but while she was packing she found that she was crying.

She wrote to Peter and posted it at Paddington Station and she put the picture of the postman toiling up the hill and across the field to the caravan to deliver it from her mind, lest she should cry again. She hailed a taxi and drove to 10 Graysmere Gardens.

It was plain from the moment she arrived that the room which would 'always be hers' was a figure of speech only. It still contained her own furniture which she had left there when she moved to Crafers, but its wardrobe housed an overflow of Diana's clothes, a motley collection ready for the jumble sale burst out of the drawers, a pile of unwanted pictures was in one corner and the whole of the floor was covered by Christopher's electric train.

"I'm terribly sorry," said Diana, "but I was out when your telegram came and I simply haven't had time to move anything. Not that there's really anywhere for it to go."

She took an armful of clothes from the wardrobe, sprinkled them with ash from her cigarette and dropped them in a pile on the bed. Loveday began to move some of the rails of the train in order to find somewhere to put her suitcases, arousing a howl from Christopher.

"Never mind, darling," said Diana cheerfully. "Aunty won't be here long. We shall be out for dinner, Loveday. What are you doing?"

"I — oh — I shall be all right."

"I mean about eating?"

"Oh."

It was clear to Loveday that she must dine out also and as soon as she had hung up some of her clothes in the vacated space in the wardrobe she went out.

It was a clear warm night and the streets were crowded with searchers after pleasure. It was the first time she had been back in London and she was at first excited and then wearied by the jostling crowds. She stood in a queue for the bus, failed to get on it, and went meekly back to the end. She had always belonged to a dismal female club, where the food was poor and the atmosphere depressing, and here she ate a solitary dinner. It was too late for the theatre, and when she toyed with the idea of going to a film, a search in the paper revealed nothing which she felt she wanted to see. There were friends she might visit, but they all seemed worlds away, and in her present mood she needed no company. Aimlessly she crossed Piccadilly and walked through Green Park. The dingy sheep lent it a rural air. She contemplated their silly faces and thought of the future.

She had no clear idea of what she wanted to do and owing to the amount of capital which she had spent on modernizing Crafers, she would find herself short of money if she had to stay in London for any length of time. She could work, of course, but it was a long time since she had done this, and years of freedom gave her a distaste for tied hours. Her slender qualifications, she knew, would debar her from anything interesting, unless she were helped by luck or influence.

She need only stay away for a month or two after all. By then her emotions would have calmed down and Peter would have forgotten her. Looking at her cottage in her mind's eye there now seemed absolutely no reason for flight. They had only each other to please. Why indeed should they not love each other as much and as deeply as this thing demanded, for the short time of happiness which it would give them.

She walked past the flower-beds and thought of the amateur beginnings of her own tiny herbaceous border and the nasturtiums she had planted to hang over the wall. Even the thought of her row of lettuce going to seed and the unpinched side-shoots of her tomatoes reproached her.

It was no good, Crafers was a place one could not shake off lightly in the way in which she had shed the thin Kensington house. As she picked her way carefully round the train system on the floor of her bedroom and moved Diana's clothes from the bed to the chair, she knew that this dignified house had never claimed her, for all the years she had lived there, as much as the ugly box which was Crafers.

The next day she was useful. Christopher had earache and without Loveday's help he might have interfered with Diana's plans. Loveday offered to stay with him and see the doctor, who expressed the opinion that it was mumps.

"Good Lord," said Diana, when she

came home. "I've never had it."

"I have," said Loveday. "Would you like to keep away? I can look after him. Mumps can be no joke when one is grown up."

Diana was not entirely heartless and moreover she was possessive about Christopher. She protested, but Alan spoke up from behind his paper.

"Best keep away or we shan't be able to go to the Slaters. I haven't had it either."

And so, during that dismal August, Loveday found herself back in the old nursery, fighting pain and boredom and fractiousness with the old tricks and special sickroom games. Christopher was not very ill, and as he sat up and looked at her steadily from under his level brows, she saw the strong family likeness to Alan, to her father, indeed to herself. If she had had a son, she thought, so might he look at her, and she was assailed with the hopeless desperation of the childless, middle-aged woman.

15

No One At Home

AT the beginning of August, Landon had to go to Belgium and Holland and took Frances with him. In their absence Julian spent an unfettered ten days with Johnny, Roberta and Ann. They washed up at queer times, made their beds just before they fell into them, and no one, except Mrs. Herbage, so much as stirred the dust, which settled gently over everything in a slum-like pall, until even Julian noticed it. At first he had felt gay and relaxed. Ann's cooking started off well, but after two days it tended to interfere with her social life and seemed to have a basic formula of baked beans. By the end of a week he was in considerable discomfort and having, until Marcy's marriage, been more or less spoilt, he was undomesticated enough not to know why.

On Saturday Julian said he would

take them all out for the day and was annoyed when Ann refused to come, without giving a reason. He did not, however, ask further and this annoyed Ann. Johnny complained that he had no clean shirt and Roberta said she had upset 'tomayto' juice all down her best frock.

"Tomahto," corrected Julian unreasonably.

"Tomahto," intoned Roberta sweetly, and Julian knew he was being tiresome and insular and rightly put in his place by a child of ten.

They went in the end, even Ann, who, after a certain amount of furtive telephoning, consented to go with them. At lunch Julian resolved to have a talk with her, but he crumbled bread and put it off, as he now put everything off, into an empty area of time, known as 'after Frances has gone'.

Some small boys in red caps came into the restaurant.

"That's my new school, Roberta," said Johnny proudly.

It occurred to Julian that the peaceful time he envisaged might even be lonely.

He looked at Ann's dark urchin beauty, at the peaked pathos of Johnny's ears, and at Roberta's gay grin showing her banded teeth and felt not paternal or avuncular, but 'motherly'. Something in him melted with pity and affection for everything that was young.

After they had spent the afternoon at a small private zoo Julian was feeling less affectionate, and to be confronted on his return home by unmade beds and unwashed dishes filled him with sudden anger.

"Ann," he said, "you're a sloven and a slut."

She looked at him open-mouthed.

"What about you?" she said evenly.

"It's not my job."

"Well, I'm — "

She paused and shook back the fringe of her hair. "You'll be telling me soon that a woman's place is in the home."

"And so," roared Julian, "it is."

"Well," said Anne again. "I never heard of anything so — "

Julian interrupted her. "Before you do another thing you go upstairs and make the beds and then wash up. Or the other way round, I don't care."

"I get your meaning," said Ann. "It might be more comfortable." At the door she paused. "And you could do the boiler. It's gone out," she added.

After Johnny and Roberta had gone to bed, Ann went across to the Hoves to look at the television and the house was still. Now, unreasonably, with the place to himself at last, Julian had a longing to bang the front door on it and go for a walk. As if sensing his restlessness, Tinker stirred at his feet and he stroked her ears to soothe her.

He had so often said hard things of women who left children alone in the house, but now he partially understood their neglect. Johnny and Roberta would doubtless sleep soundly enough not to miss him if he went out, but duty chained him to the house, and at last, resenting the past, the present and the future, he went to bed.

His sister returned the following day, having left Landon in London, and Julian always suppressed a guilty relief when his brother-in-law did not appear. He found he had surges of affection for his relations only when they were not there. While Frances was still at that stage of standing about with her hat in her hand and saying she simply must unpack, Ann burst in, followed by two young men.

"I say," she said. "I've brought Theo and Archie in to supper. There is some food, I saw it, a big bit of ham. Marcy brought it. Jack killed a pig."

She introduced everyone with artless inelegance.

"Daddy, this is Theo. This is Archie. This is my American Aunt I told you about. May we have some drinks?"

The two youths came forward, thanked Julian for the sherry he poured out and called him 'Sir'. Ann turned on the radio, Johnny and Roberta scrapped in a corner and Frances began to talk gaily and loudly, her slight American accent suddenly noticeable. Julian decided against a drink, though at the moment mild intoxication seemed the only way of passing the evening in less than misery. Then he thought of Loveday Flayne. He saw in his mind's eye her box of a cottage walled in with silence. He had no desire to marry her, or indeed to marry anyone, but after an assault had been made on the ham and Roberta and Johnny had gone protesting to bed, he left the party playing Canasta and, taking the dogs, walked up the hill in the general direction of Crafers. He really had no intention of calling, and yet half an hour later he was knocking at her door.

There was no answer and he was unreasonably disappointed. He walked round the house for a sign of life, thinking she might be in the garden using the last of the light, and also remembering that she had once said she could not hear the front door when she was at the back of the house, for, small though it was, its walls were thick. He turned as he heard a footstep and fixed his gaze on Peter, now leaning over the field gate and looking at Julian with equal ferocity.

"Hallo," said Julian. "How are you now? Better?"

"Yes, thanks."

"I — I was looking for Miss Flayne. Is she away?"

"She is."

"Oh! For long?"

"I don't know. She — she just packed up and went."

He picked up a fir cone, turned round and threw it with violence as far as he could. It disturbed the starlings in the copse and they flew out of the trees, blackening the sky with a whirr of wings.

"Oh — well — " said Julian, "perhaps someone was ill. I suppose you're keeping an eye on the place for her. Lonely up here, isn't it?"

"Loveday and I like it," said Peter, glaring across the field at the trees blurred in the dusk. He looked ill, Julian thought, as he opened the gate and walked into the field.

"I'll go home this way. Tinker prefers it, don't you, young lady," said Julian.

Tinker and Lob, released from their leads, sped away after a rabbit.

"Well — I must be going — er — Good-night."

The young man's unblinking stare confused Julian. He walked off across the field, wondering why it was that he found the young man so infuriating. And he called her 'Loveday' too.

A week later he called again. He knew that Loveday was in London for Mrs. Spracker told Mrs. Livers and Mrs. Livers told Marcy, but he thought Peter might have more exact news.

The shut windows made the lonely little house as hostile as a fortress. He turned and then noticed that the caravan was no longer there either. Sheep were nibbling at the flattened square of anaemic grass. There were the remains of a small fire and charred pieces of paper blew in the wind. There was now, realized Julian, no excuse whatever for him to take this steep walk again. He wondered why he had done it so often and could find no reasonable answer.

16

The Letter

FROM her leper's window Loveday watched Diana, vivid and lovely, departing for all the gaieties of that Coronation year, and was suddenly warmed and comforted by the thought that Peter loved her.

Christopher was up again and Diana was safely out of quarantine when his letter came. It was addressed to Crafers and had been re-directed in the upright hand of Mr. Piper, the postmaster.

My very dearest (she read)
I believe you will get this if I send it to Crafers. Indeed, I know that if I stood old Piper a drink he would give me your address. As it is, don't ask me how I know you are in London — I do, but I won't be the pest I realize you think me and pursue you further.
This is just to tell you that you can

298

come back because I have taken up my bed and walked away. I shan't tell you where — I can have secrets too.

She turned over the envelope and saw the postmark was S.W.1. He must be quite near somewhere, lost in that swarm of human beings.

I enclose a cutting which I thought might amuse you.

She looked at the cutting. It was from *The Sunday Sun*, a picture of an unphotogenic woman, surrounded by eight children of various sizes, and by her side a grinning youth with his hand on her shoulder. Underneath were the words: 'Michael Splice, aged nineteen, weds mother of eight — says you're as old as you feel.'

'Well,' thought Loveday, folding the cutting, 'he certainly looks pleased enough with his bride.' She wondered how they both might feel in twenty years' time, and she wished she could shake off the feeling that even by so much as being seen with Peter, now that they were in love with each other, she was making them both ridiculous. She was conventional enough to hate this, apart from the fact that she felt there was something unnatural about any relationship between them.

The letter went on:

> *You are really better looking than Mrs. Splice, you haven't eight children, so there is every excuse for me — if not for Michael.*
>
> *I didn't mean to stray into forbidden fields, only to tell you all the news. I cut your hedge for you before I left. The lettuces have gone to seed.* (I thought they would, sighed Loveday.) *Now I come to think of it there is no news — I typed for three days and nights almost without stopping and Malayan Episode has gone to meet its fate. Now I feel sort of purged and light-headed.*
>
> *I won't pretend I don't miss you and long to see you again. I can't really see why you ran away. If you love me a bit, as I almost believe you did, everything was made perfect. Forbidden talk again,*
>
> Your
Peter.

There was no address, yet she was tempted to reply, as he had done, through the medium of Mr. Piper, and a few days later she wrote him a short impersonal note, wishing him luck with his book. When she came back from posting it she felt as if she had buried a body, and yet here they both were in London Postal District S.W.1 — maybe even next door to each other — she found herself turning her head if she saw a fair head or heard a deep laugh.

* * *

The evening was drenched by a sudden summer storm and the rain ran down the gutters splashing her stockings. It was dirty, smut-laden rain. Inadequately equipped Londoners sprang dripping into taxis or lurked in doorways looking up for a break in the clouds. She thought of the earthy smell of her garden, of the drenching gusts blowing across the hill, of the leaky spot under the roof where she had to keep a tin bowl, of the misery of fetching coal in the rain, of her Wellingtons standing under the sink ready for action.

With fierce longing she walked briskly back to Graysmere Gardens, filled with the energy born of resolve. She would go back to Crafers tomorrow by the first train. The plans began to work in her brain. She would send Mrs. Spracker a telegram, she would telephone the tradesmen from the box at the corner, she would buy some food at Harrods before she started. She would . . . Why, she had been crazy to leave Crafers. Now when she looked back the reason seemed totally inadequate.

She opened the front door with her latch-key. From the small drawing-room on the left came Diana's voice, high and laughing. As she took a step up the stair to avoid losing time, for her mind was far away on time-tables, packing, and emergency ration cards, the door opened and Diana called her name.

"Loveday — here's a friend of yours. I've been entertaining him, but I simply must fly now. You'll be in, won't you, to listen to Christopher? It's Trudi's night off."

She opened the door wider and made

302

a polite farewell to the man standing by the fire-place.

It was Peter.

He stood quite still looking at Loveday steadily with no hint of a smile and she moved slowly across the room, her mackintosh dripping unpardonably on the honey-coloured carpet. She was so glad to see Peter that complete happiness engulfed her and drained away all reasonable thought.

"I — I've just written to you," she said.

"Have you?"

He held out both his hands and took one of hers and stroked it gently.

"How did you know I was here?" she asked.

"I've known all the time."

She looked startled.

"Yes, I have," he went on. "It was really too simple. I knew you had gone to London, so I guessed you might be at your brother's. I looked him up in the telephone book, and rang up and said I was Harrods and wanted to speak to you about a fitting. If you had been there I planned to ring off. A voice said you were out, so I knew you were there. I didn't mean to bother you, but I like to know where you are. It made me unhappy not knowing. Don't do it again. And I haven't bothered you, have I?"

"No," Loveday smiled.

He helped her off with her mackintosh and she sat down.

"But today — " she spread out her hands, laughing. "What has brought you here today?"

"Oh, that? Do you know, darling, I'm so excited — no, not exactly excited, but so perfectly blissful at seeing you, I'd forgotten."

He seemed to take a short journey away from her, considering what had brought him here in the end. She thought, looking at him, that he looked older, more purposeful —

"Loveday, imagine — the oddest thing — they've taken my book."

She gave a cry of pleasure and jumped up.

"Really, but how wonderful! How simply marvellous! Congratulations! Tell me about it — everything. How did it happen?"

"I can't believe it even now. A chap I know advised me to send my manuscript to an agent instead of direct to Blair and Woods, as I had planned, and so I did, and the very next week they sent for me and told me they thought they could place it for me with Green and Fenton's if I'd re-write two of the chapters. So I sat up all one night and did that, and they took it. I've just heard. Of course the contract isn't signed and it all takes time, but, Loveday, I'm so thrilled. Do you know," he paused and tugged his hair and clenched his teeth, idiotic in his excitement, "Fallow, the agent, thinks it might go in America and even make a film. I'll be rich. You'll see — " he sobered for a moment. "I'm bound to say though, that at the moment I shall be lucky if I get an advance of fifty pounds."

Loveday laughed at his happy transition from flights of fancy to reality.

"The money is really the least part, isn't it?" she said in her gentle voice.

"Yes," he said. "Funny, isn't it, because I could so well do with it. And yet it is the least part. But I can make more. I can be a writer. It — it just opens a way into the sort of country where I want to live."

"A lonely country," said Loveday.

"Is it?"

"I've always thought it must be."

"Maybe you're right. I'm a lonely person anyway."

He put his hands gently on her shoulders and looked at her.

"Wasn't it fun at Overbridge?" he said. "Can't we go back?"

She shook her head, but even the slight contact of his hands on her shoulders stirred her.

"Peter, don't, darling, don't. I've tried to explain. I suppose it's partly vanity. I can't see myself as one of those laughable types who chase after boys like you. It — it seems almost immoral to me."

"I'm not a boy, and now you see, darling, I can marry you."

"Marry me!"

"Don't be shocked at such a respectable suggestion."

"I — but my dear, that would be worse, tying you up irrevocably to someone who will be an old woman in no time."

"Let's not think of that time," he said.

"Let's not think of marriage," she answered.

She was deeply moved at the thought, ridiculous though it was. She saw rows of faces the faces of friends, Janet, her brother: 'My dear, she's old enough to be his mother,' and then suddenly she found she was near tears. She hadn't cried for years until she met Peter, she thought viciously, as she caught her trembling lip in her teeth to steady herself.

"Don't cry, darling," he said softly, "There's nothing to cry about."

She managed to smile at last.

"I don't want to keep on, Loveday, but I've made a perfectly honourable proposal. I can't see what there is in it to make you cry."

"I'm not crying now."

She gave a final sniff, fearful of the havoc tears can wreak on the appearance of even the young and beautiful.

"About marrying me," persisted Peter.

Loveday interrupted him: "It's not to be thought of," she said harshly. "I couldn't be as selfish as that, however

307

much I — I want you."

"And you do — want me?" He put his arms around her shoulders. She could feel the quivering tension of his body. Suddenly she felt she had only one duty — that there was no longer any question of right or wrong, of convention or prudence. She had to stop the torment of this boy and there was only one way, even if she was the one who could not fail to lose.

"I will live with you," she said in a precise voice, "until you are tired of me — and then — I would leave you free for someone of your own age."

He drew away and regarded her with a long stare and she saw to her amazement that she had shocked him.

"I don't want just that," he said, "I want to marry you, to have you for always. I — I couldn't bear anything else."

He stood up and looked down on her, all passion gone.

"Don't you understand?" he said.

She nodded. "I'm beginning to."

"It's no good my saying I won't see you again, because I have to, now and then, but I won't bother you. I'll try not to anyway," then he broke out again. "Damnation, Loveday, why can't you marry me?"

So swiftly does the mood change in love or what passes for it she was startled by a feeling of irritation.

"I've told you," she said impatiently. "Just our ages? No one else, nothing else?"

"No!"

"I see — "

He looked unbearably young, all his jaunty self-possession gone, his hair ruffled in his excitement out of its unusual sleekness into the familiar tuft at the back. Even his elegant town clothes seemed as if the pockets were weighted by his misery. Then he looked up at her with such an air of desperation that she felt she must do anything, anything he asked to protect him from the useless anguish she herself had known.

"Peter — be sensible — believe me when I say you — we — shall get over this — one does, you know — things don't last."

"They couldn't," he said gruffly,

making for the door, "if they did, I should die."

He stood at the door and she stayed at the fireplace, separated by space — by time — by generation. From outside came voices.

"What are you going to do, my dear? Can't you be sensible?"

"No," he said fiercely. "I'm going to get drunk."

He opened the door, nearly knocking down Alan who was about to come in, and with no farewells he was gone.

17

Journey

WHILE Loveday was deciding to catch the afternoon train Frances Grove was looking at the back of the neck of the woman in front of her at the counter at Cook's in Berkeley Street, and registering unconsciously the knowledge that she was an American, even before she opened her mouth. The woman began to talk and Frances recognized a mid-western accent. A wave of longing swept over her for her own apartment in New York, and just as all those months before she had yearned for crumpets by the open fire, soft English voices, the green cosiness, the solidity, the restraint of England, so now she was irked by it. She wanted — how could she explain what she wanted, when she knew even now that it would melt in her fingers like an icicle the moment she grasped it. It was the penalty of the migrant. Roberta was free of it, Landon had been free of it for four generations, but she had two souls and they left her body at different times for different reasons.

The clerk, who lived at Forest Hill and had never been farther from England than Northern France in 1940, handed over the tickets as if he were a bus conductor giving her a threepenny fare. The man behind her moved up.

★ ★ ★

She no longer took a taxi automatically but walked briskly in the sunshine with the stride she had used as a girl, down Berkeley Street, across Piccadilly and the Green Park, to the Mall. In front of the Palace was a small crowd, women in light frocks, a clergyman, two schoolgirls. As she wondered what they should be waiting for, there was a stir amongst them and a car drove out of the gate and down Constitution Hill. Inside was a small yellow-haired Prince and a baby Princess, imperious in her nurse's lap, waving with calm politeness to the crowd. Everything about

312

the equipage was immaculate, polished, shining. Frances waved excitedly and when the car vanished she let her hand fall and felt slightly ridiculous. The crowd melted away. She caught the clergyman's eye and smiled. For the moment she had forgotten she was now an American.

"I feel," said the clergyman, "that they're the only thing worth fighting for."

"I know what you mean," said Frances. "If there were ever a revolution I'd hide them in oak trees all over the place."

"Bonnie Prince Charlie," said the clergyman.

"Poor little boy," said Frances.

The clergyman raised his hat, suddenly embarrassed that he had spoken to a strange woman, and walked quickly down the Mall. They were taking down the entrancing arches and for a moment Frances stood looking after his retreating figure, trying to recall the triumphal pageantry of the Coronation and wondering when she would see London again. Now she saw New York only with the distaste of an exile, uncomforted by air-conditioning or the perfection of her kitchen and bathrooms. Her mind made winged flights between the countries. Who was it had said: 'American life is glossy, and English life is glowing.' With fanfare of trumpets echoing in her ears she hailed a taxi to catch the afternoon train to Overbridge.

★ ★ ★

Loveday tipped the porter and settled herself in a corner seat. The train was nearly empty and she saw Frances sweep past her down the platform with something forceful about her gait, her neat shoes, her constricted bosom. After some minutes she came back to the bookstall, and it was thus that she saw Loveday, whom she greeted with the enthusiasm of the woman who cannot bear to be alone with herself. She used the few minutes before the train started to have her luggage moved into Loveday's compartment, and with a start Loveday realized that she had jettisoned a first-class ticket for the sake of her company.

She sat in the corner opposite, obviously prepared, Loveday realized not without horror, to talk for the whole of the journey.

"You have been away?" was her opening remark.

"Yes," answered Loveday.

"Holiday?"

"No," replied Loveday in an uncommunicative tone. But it was no good. Frances would have extracted the plans of a Carmelite nun and Loveday found herself saying: "I've been at my brother's in London. My nephew had mumps."

"Oh! So that's why you dashed off so suddenly?"

It was convenient to let Frances think this was the reason, and she nodded.

"We missed you."

"I don't believe it," laughed Loveday.

"But we did. Marcy wondered why you weren't at the Women's Institute and Johnny kept asking when you were going to let him have some more stamps."

"Poor lamb. I did promise him some. I had forgotten."

"And I believe my brother walked up one evening, but no one was there."

"How is he — Johnny, I mean?" asked Loveday.

"Oh, quite fit really. He is going away to school in the autumn."

"Yes, I knew."

"You did?" There was a slightly surprised arching of Frances' thin eyebrows.

"Yes. Your brother told me. I met him in Avonbury Spa the day he had been to see the school."

"Oh."

Frances sighed. She wished she could explain how she longed to marry her brother off before she left England and what hopes she had had of Loveday being just the person. She thought Loveday was very like the woman she herself might have been had she not married an American, and this gave her a feeling of sympathy. This was, however, not reciprocated by Loveday, who wanted nothing more than to look out of the window in a sort of coma of mental fatigue.

Francis' bright voice ran on. "I hope to take Ann back with me. It will do her such a lot of good and she'll be company

316

for Roberta. We're going back by boat — on the *Caronia*. My husband has to fly, but England must have slowed me up or something. I guess I'd rather go by boat."

She laughed as if she were confessing to some old-fashioned prejudice.

Loveday disciplined her thoughts and struggled into the conversation.

★ ★ ★

With forethought she had ordered young Bentley's taxi by telegram and she therefore refused the offer of a lift from Julian, who had come to meet Frances. The sight of so many people whom she knew and who greeted her by name, young Ernie, the stationmaster, and a grubby boy who took her ticket, as well as a cool smile from Julian, gave her a feeling of homecoming, almost as if they were members of a loving family waiting on the steps of the ancestral home to welcome the traveller. She asked Bentley to stop at Mrs. Spracker's, and here she found that all her movements were known, for Mrs. Spracker's sister

Ada's girl was married to the milkman, who had been instructed to leave a pint of milk.

"It's all aired," said Mrs. Spracker, and I've left you some eggs. I've been in every week. My Dolly popped up in between and put a bottle in the bed. But the garden's in a fine old mess. You can leave a house or a husband, but you can't never leave a garden," added Mrs. Spracker reproachfully.

She spoke no more than the truth and before Loveday had unpacked properly she found herself weeding. She started by pulling up a few docks by the front door, but twilight found her cutting back neglected plants and planning great things for the next day. When darkness chased her indoors she boiled an egg and opened the Parish Magazine. She read of the christening of Marilyn Sheila Betts, the long-awaited daughter of the policeman after a row of sons, and saw that old Mrs. Leigh had died at last. The vicar was happy to report that the Tower fund now stood at three hundred and ninety pounds.

Since she came to live in Overbridge

nearly fifty pounds had been collected, she wished suddenly that she were rich enough to buy the vicar his tower and yet, she thought, as she shut the Parish Magazine and put it on one side to pass on to Mrs. Spracker, if all these small efforts were not needed, a good deal of interest would be lost to the village, no fêtes, no bring-and-buys, no jumble sales. She yawned and, pleasantly weary, she went to bed and slept soundly.

18

Up The Hill

BEFORE they left Europe, Frances and Landon were planning a visit to Paris to be followed by a lightning brush with Italy and, when Frances came back from London full of hotel and plane reservations, Friar's House was filled with the scurry of their plans.

"I went to see that vixen of a grandmother of Ann's, old Mrs. Forstal, while I was in London," said Frances.

"What on earth for? I thought you couldn't stand her."

"Nor can I. What's more, she doesn't improve."

"Well, why on earth?"

"It was about Ann. I want to take her with me to Paris."

"Well, that's all right. I said she could go."

"But I also want to take her back with

me to the States, and I thought I'd better sound the old lady. I thought she might disgorge the fare. And this morning I've had a letter to say she will."

"Really, Frances, what an idea! Why didn't you ask me?"

"Because I don't believe you could afford it. Now, be honest, can you?"

"Not easily, with Johnny off to school, though of course I'd try. But do you think it's a good idea?"

"Yes, I do. It was the making of me. Look at me. If I'd never gone to the States I'd look like — like Marcy."

Julian laid his penetrating gaze on his sister. Her clothes sat well on a good foundation garment inside which was constricting her plumpening body. There was a briskness, a tension about her which made for a gaiety which was attractive but restless. Julian sighed and wondered what improvements Ann would receive.

He only said: "We should miss her," considering without rancour the complete disruption of the last six months of his life and seeing the future as a shifting, unpleasant thing. He thought, as he did so often at this time of day, that he would feel better if he had a large gin.

Frances had been to tea with Marcy and had been fetched by Julian on his return. She had found an empty house and two notes. One in the kitchen said: *Done potaters and spare room. paid meat kindly order black lead and oblidge Mrs. Herbage.*

The other propped up by the sitting-room clock, said tersely: *Taken kids to Lambe's. Back sevenish. Ann.*

At the thought of black lead Frances shuddered. It was like ordering rushes and candles. What a country!

What a kitchen! She too thought of a drink with a certain pleasure and she carried the tray of bottles into the sitting-room before she took off her hat. It was cool and rather dark. What it wanted was a window looking to the south. She never came into any room in the house without longing to set about it with a pick-axe. And yet — she knew not why — she loved it all.

Brother and sister let the alcohol comfort them for their various reasons. To Julian the future acquired stability, and Frances found herself minding the kitchen stove and the hole in the carpet less violently.

"I planned to get you married before I went home," she said, her tongue indiscreetly oiled by a second gin.

"What, me?"

Julian sat up and glared at his sister with his misleading violence. "Won't you ever realize, woman, that I don't want to get married again?"

"But I can't go back and leave you in this chaos. Mrs. Herbage means well enough but the house will be filthy in no time."

"I shall be all right. I can eat out. Johnny will be at school."

"But he'll be home all the holidays."

"We can both eat out. Anyhow, I can cook."

"You'll be hideously uncomfortable."

"I shan't."

"And who will look after him while you are at the office?"

"He can go to the Lambe's or Marcy might have him."

"How will he get over there?"

"I could drive him."

Julian thought of the future after his second gin as something rather peaceful with all the difficulties overcome, the house to himself, no noise, no turmoil.

Frances continued in a depressing voice: "Supposing Johnny is ill."

"Ah yes! Supposing."

At the moment he felt sure that Johnny wasn't going to be ill again — ever — but reason at last prevailed and he gave a deep sigh.

"I travelled home with Miss Flayne. She has been away looking after her brother's boy. If you had any sense I could have married you both off by now," said Frances.

"Indeed?"

"Yes, Marcy and I decided she would do quite nicely, but you're just obstinate."

He laughed, not considering for a moment that they were serious, and then suddenly Frances leaned forward and became, as she did momentarily now and then, the dearly loved companion of his younger self.

"Really, Julian, couldn't you try to like her?"

"I do like her — very much."

"Well then — "

"One needs more than that."

"Not at your age."

He laughed again: "You'd be surprised what one can want," he raised his eyebrows, "at my age. I agree she's a charming person. I like her, but she simply doesn't stir me further at all and I don't think that would make either of us happy. And she might not like me."

"No, perhaps not," said Frances.

She, too, now felt relaxed and happy. She really couldn't worry any more about Julian. If he wasn't going to marry again he'd just have to sell Friar's House and live in a hotel. She made this suggestion.

"I suppose I could," he said, and from the tone of his voice she knew he would do no such thing and they sat in silence until the door crashed open with the children's return.

★ ★ ★

From the moment Ann was told that she could go to New York with her aunt she became vaguely transatlantic. Frances took her to Avonbury to by her some new clothes with a cheque from Julian. Henry and Robin showed gratifying sorrow that she was going so far away and she said, with gay confidence, that she would see them when she came back in the spring. She was dizzy with thoughts of a vast continent inhabited by the counterpart of Gregory Peck, and she sloughed off her English admirers like a snake shedding its skin. Julian was glad of Henry's eclipse, but he was sorry for Robin, who journeyed all the way to Overbridge to give her a small golden heart for her charm bracelet. But she was now the responsibility of Frances and he sighed with relief.

Marcy had undertaken to buy Johnny's school outfit and piles of clothes waiting to be marked with Cash's name-tapes were on the study chairs. Ann swirled new skirts and preened under new hats. Roberta was measured for an English flannel suit and Johnny stood about with a serious face trying on red blazers a size too large.

'It was,' thought Julian, 'like Marcy's wedding, only worse.'

★ ★ ★

A week later, in a mood of desperation which he did not pretend to understand, he took the car and set off to give Loveday a proposal of marriage.

"There's no doubt about it," he said to Frances before he set out, "I'm just not proof against nagging women. You and Marcy have nagged me into this — on your heads be it."

"Oh, Julian, we haven't nagged you. We just think you ought to be married. And really, this Flayne woman is heaven-sent. She's just the person. I thought so from the moment I saw her. And at your age you can't really expect to be as uncritically in love as you were with Judy."

"No, thank heavens, but I'm not in love at all, which is a disadvantage, you must admit."

"She's a most attractive woman."

"I know."

"Couldn't you work yourself up a bit

about her?" said Frances.

"Oh, I like her, I like her immensely, but I'd have to be honest with her. I'd have to say it was really just a housekeeper-companion I want and — "

Frances almost screamed with impatience. "Then you won't get her. A woman like Loveday Flayne isn't going to look at such a proposition."

"Well, what do I do? Swear undying love?" He knocked his pipe out on the fireplace. "All right, I'll do it, I'll do it now, and she'll say 'No' and then I hope everyone will be happy."

With some misgivings Frances heard him go into the yard of the Duke's Head to get out the car. She wished she could fetch him back and groom him for the occasion. He had shaved badly that morning, his shirt cuffs were frayed and the stuffing was coming out of his tie.

She was like a film director faced with inadequate actors. If only they would do exactly as she said, if only she could speak for them, breathe for them, wear their clothes, everything would be well, but they moved stiffly under her directions like puppets, and she could not communicate the wisdom and judgement that was in her to their dumb spirits. That it was wisdom and judgement she never questioned.

★ ★ ★

Loveday had found that the days melted into each other until she almost forgot that she had been away. There was a great deal to do in house and garden and Mrs. Livers had only to see smoke coming through her chimney to rush up with eggs and a request 'to give her a hand with the whist drive.' A note from the G.P.O. indicated that the telephone would be installed the following week, and Loveday was suddenly connected with the world. On her hilltop she could look down on the lights of Overbridge and feel god-like and free, or lonely, according to her mood. Few people knocked at her door, excusing themselves if she met them in the village 'because of the hill'.

The autumn made amends for the wet summer and the days were so bright and warm that she was surprised to see gold in the leaves, and to find nuts and acorns ripening, in a landscape which daily grew more rich and splendid. It was just a year since old Miss Cox had died and she had first come to Overbridge, and she thought over the past months with a feeling of disbelief that she was the same person. Though sometimes she wondered uneasily what had happened to Peter she could now laugh gently at herself, not without a feeling of gratitude that she should have been loved and that she had escaped. She pushed the episode into a sort of lumber room in her mind, which contained unwanted experiences she strove to forget. At night, when the bats scurried through the darkness and the lights in the village went out one by one, she would wish for many things which she could not put into words, and though she was convinced her decision was right, the thought of Peter would stir her heart and make her restless.

★ ★ ★

When Julian drove up she was tying back some ramblers, scratched to the elbows, hot and untidy, and she was pleased to find that he did not immediately tell her that what she was doing was quite wrong. What visitors she had showed a distressing tendency to give gardening advice, which Loveday found conflicted with each other and with the three gardening books from which she tried to learn, and though the prospect of a visitor filled her with less enthusiasm than usual because she realize that she had no cigarettes, she welcomed him gaily and made no apologies.

He was a man with a burden lying so visibly on his mind that she began to wonder if there was some hitch about Johnny's school.

"Do you mind if I smoke a pipe?" he said at length. "Johnny? Oh, he's all right. Goes to school next week, and Frances and Roberta leave in October, with Ann, you know."

"So you will be all alone?"

Here was the opening. He suppressed an inward grin at the thought that he now ought to go down one one knee and while he was considering this the telephone rang. Loveday dealt audibly with this interruption. It was about a rehearsal of the Overbridge Players.

"Life was a good deal more peaceful before I had the telephone," she said. "That was Mrs. Fanshawe. They're doing *Dear Octopus*, you know."

Julian nodded.

"And the girl who is playing Cynthia, do you remember?"

Julian nodded again, and added a small sound not unlike a grunt to reinforce his assent.

"Well, Celia Payne is doing the part, but she can't play the piano, so I have to do it 'off', while she goes through the motions. It's terribly complicated, and more or less all done by mirrors and timing and hoarse whispers."

"It will be all right on the night."

"I wish I thought so."

"Always is," Julian puffed away. "What is it you have to play? I forget."

"That bit out of the 'Kerry Dancers'. Don't you remember? 'Oh! The song of the Kerry dancers; Oh! The sound of the piper's tune.' It always makes me feel about ninety, but it's so touching."

"Do you dance?"

"Hardly ever now, and the significant

thing about it is that I don't mind."

She laughed.

"The consolations of middle age."

With horror he stopped speaking. The mention of middle age could hardly be a good preliminary to a proposal of marriage and he searched in his mind for a subject to bring the conversation to a more inspiring level. A silence stretched between them.

He had always been so easy to entertain that Loveday was puzzled and she filled the void by suggesting a cup of tea. As she drew the water at the sink she looked gratefully out of the tiny window which framed the corner of the field. Every job in this cottage had its compensations. As one washed up one saw a small Corot; getting in the coal at sunset became a spreading Turner, and making the beds gave one a complete Rowland Hilder across the tree-edged fields to the farm roofs belows.

She looked out automatically while the kettle boiled and then drew a quick breath, for there, in its old patch by the copse, was the splash of Peter's car and the caravan, and when she carried the tray back to the sitting-room she found she was trembling a little.

Julian was standing by the fireplace, knocking out his pipe. He looked up at her, with an air of desperation.

"I came here to ask you to marry me," he said, his words clipped and formal, and almost devoid of feeling.

She put down the tray to the jingle of china, as her hands shook. Words stuck in her throat.

"I — I never thought of such a thing."

He still looked deadly solemn.

"Please consider it," he said.

Suddenly she began to laugh. "But, my dear man, what a way to propose!"

She held up the teapot, momentarily recovered. She could still see, from the corner window, the edge of Peter's caravan.

"Do you take sugar?" she asked.

"No — I mean, no thank you. What was wrong with my proposal?"

"Everything," said Loveday; "but it doesn't matter. The answer is 'No'."

Instead of the surge of relief which he had anticipated he found himself flung down with disappointment. As she handed him the tea, with the small one-sided smile he liked so much, he saw all prospect of the calm peace which he longed for in his life, floating away, and leaving him in some dark chaos. He was about to speak again, hurriedly, without considering his words, when there was a resounding knock on the back door.

"Oh dear," apologized Loveday. "I go days without seeing anybody except the baker, and then all my visitors come at once."

She was hardly in the kitchen when the latch was lifted and Peter reached the sitting-room in what seemed like a couple of bounds.

"Loveday, Loveday darling. Think of it," he said, barely nodding at Julian. Indeed, although he saw him quite plainly, he was so excited that Julian seemed outside what he was doing, as if he were separated by a glass wall.

"They want to make a film of my book. Did you ever?"

"No," echoed Loveday. "My dear, how wonderful."

She held out both her hands and Peter

took them and whirled her round so that in the confined space she almost knocked Julian's tea out of his hand.

"Peter. It's wonderful, but do calm down. Say 'How do you do' to Mr. Lenham like a civilized being."

"How do you do, Sir," said Peter.

Julian, while deploring the general lack of manners in the young, was jolted, as always, when he was called 'Sir'.

"I don't know what this is all about," he said, "but I am sure I must congratulate you."

"You must indeed," said Loveday, pushing back a curl of hair. "He has written a book, and it has been taken in America, and now they want to make a film of it."

She looked proudly at Peter as if she herself had some part in his triumph.

"Fetch your cup and I'll give you some tea, if is hasn't all gone," she added.

Peter walked to the cupboard and brought forth his own outsize cup, took the teapot from Loveday's hand and helped himself lavishly to sugar, talking the whole time as if the older man had not been there. Julian was not offended

336

by such neglect, for he was familiar with the role of spectator, but now he wished passionately that this boy would depart and this he showed no signs of doing. He was irritated by his long strand of hair, his self-assurance, his youth, irritated by his calm possession of Loveday.

She was now kneeling, putting a match to the fire. The dry twigs crackled, giving sudden friendliness to the room, and Julian found that he was reluctant to leave. The thought crept into his mind and lingered there, that to be married to a woman like Loveday might open a world of comforting happiness. Despair laid hold of him that he had not realized this before.

He rose. "I suppose I shall see you at *Dear Octopus*," he said.

Loveday took him to the door and found his hat and stick.

"You'll hardly see me. I'm only 'noises off', you know."

"Marcy is sure to bring in some people after it is all over. I — I hope you will be one of them."

She opened the door and began to walk down the path with him. In the excitement of Peter's arrival until this moment she had forgotten that only a short while ago she had refused to marry him. Embarrassment clipped her speech.

"I don't know at all what will be happening," she said shortly.

"I — I feel that I may not have put my — my case very well," he said. "Perhaps another day I could re-open the subject."

"I shouldn't, if I were you," said Loveday cheerfully.

She could hear the voice of Jimmy Edwards issuing from the cottage. Peter had evidently turned on the radio.

She held out her hand: "Let's forget about it," she said. "Good-night."

As he shut the gate between them she looked at him, half-laughing, half-tender, and he heard her quick steps up the path.

He did not drive straight home.

★ ★ ★

With the ruthlessness of a general asking for news of battle, Frances, who had been

338

waiting for him, gave a long questioning "We — ell" before he was through the door.

"She wouldn't have me," he announced.

"Oh, Julian, you are so dumb," said his sister, impatience in her voice. "I suppose you botched it?"

"Yes," said Julian wearily. "That's about it," and he went slowly up the stairs.

19

Farewells

DURING the month before the Overbridge Players produced *Dear Octopus* there was a rehearsal twice a week. Some of these took place in the play-room at Friar's House, because the Memorial Hall was engaged every Monday by the British Legion and every Friday for a Grand Half-crown Ball with Len Cant's Band from Hinwood; not to mention the annual general meeting of the Conservative Association and the Parish Social. Loveday hoped fervently that she would not see Julian, but when her hopes were realized she found that she was disappointed, for, without Julian's drooping figure, all his pockets apparently loaded with heavy objects and his fierce eye and mild laugh, Friar's House somehow lost its spirit, and although Loveday saw Frances walking about with a business-like air, she no more belonged to Friar's House than the Overbridge Players. One evening Johnny crept in and stood by her side at the old piano, quite still, watching and listening, glorious in the new red of St. Martin's, Avonbury. When he volunteered the information that he was going to school the next day and after that his father was going away to fish, the rehearsals seemed less interesting, wherever they were held.

★ ★ ★

Peter was in London again. The empty caravan was still in its corner looking without its owner, like some forgotten toy, but he had been back scarcely long enough to startle her and interrupt her peace when he decided to return. The acceptance of his book in some way changed him, and though his youthful egotism remained undiminished, there was a confidence about him now which made him quieter. He only once spoke about his feelings for her, saying lightly:

"I won't bother you. Don't send me away."

341

He had said this before, but this time he apparently meant it, or perhaps, thought Loveday, the violence of his feeling had gone. Neither of them spoke of it, indeed they now talked of nothing which did not inevitably lead back to *Malayan Episode* and Loveday offered to help him with the proofs, for she had had some experience of this.

On the morning in October of the dress rehearsal of *Dear Octopus* in the Memorial Hall, Peter called to Loveday over the wall.

"I say, I've got to go to London. Tell the milkman, there's a dear."

He sat on the wall and picked at the stonecrop along its edge. The morning sun was treacherously bright.

"Will you miss me, Loveday?"

"Of course."

"I'll bet."

He dropped his feet on to the path.

"I'm making some coffee. Come and have a cup."

She seldom went near his caravan. Since his illness some still conventional caution had kept her away, but now she said: "That's kind. I'd love to."

She washed her hands and put on her Wellingtons, for the field was only half grazed and the clover held the dew. At the entrance she pulled them off and then sat on his bunk seat with her stockinged feet tucked under her. The air was coffee-scented. He made it simply in a large jug and poured it into two beer mugs with badly printed pictures of the Queen across them.

"The Livers' farewell present," he said.

"Farewell?"

She had sent him away so often and said 'Good-bye' to him, hoping she had seen the last of him, that she was unprepared for the knell of the word 'Farewell'.

"I'm selling the van to Don and Marjorie Sellinge. They came to stay at Easter. Remember? They've got nowhere to live in the vacations. He's up at Cambridge, you know, and they haven't a bean and Don can do casual work for the Livers, just as I did. They will be much better neighbours than I am. You'll like Marjorie, she's quiet and awfully sensible and Don hardly ever speaks. They're just the sort of people you like."

"How do you know what kind of people I like?"

"I know you pretty well, Loveday. You've hated my noise and the way I walk in and out."

"But I haven't, indeed you're wrong."

"I'm not wrong. I wanted so terribly to make you like me — love me — and I've done everything possible from the moment I arrived to make myself a nuisance, even the bucket of water."

"Oh, Peter, spare me that bucket of water."

It had served them as a joke for so long that Loveday was surprised when she found she had no desire to laugh, that indeed she was near to tears. She caressed the large mug she held in her hand, and spoke hastily of other things. They did not tell each other that the urgency of passion between them had gone, for there was no need. They both knew it. They sat on either side of the caravan drinking out of hideous Coronation mugs, calm, solemn and rather sad.

"Loveday — "

"Mm."

She looked across at him with the

expression of transparent candour which made her many friends.

"I want to talk to you."

"Well, so you are."

She knew what he was going to say and there was a strange emptiness in her heart. She felt suddenly cold, mentally and physically, and she gave a little shiver and put her hand across her breast and drew her jersey together as if she wanted to make herself smaller.

"I know," she said, "that you've come to your senses — and I'm awfully glad."

"Are you? I don't know that I am. I loved being in a turmoil about you." He thrust his hand through his hair, once again too long. "But it was awfully exhausting."

"For both of us," she added. "It's better that it should be over."

The peace around her became loneliness again. She looked back across the months and heard nothing but laughter and voices high in argument.

"You've taught me so many things, Loveday," Peter continued. "If I live to be an old, old man with a long beard I shan't forget you. I thought you were awfully cruel not to marry me, but I can see now that you were right really. Later on perhaps I'll find someone I'll like enough to marry and have rows of children."

A knife turned in her heart at the thought of children.

"But I'll always have a — a loving feeling about you — it's hard to describe."

"Better put it in a book," laughed Loveday, placing her empty mug on the locker beside her and preparing to go.

He looked over her head through the little window and saw the square box of bricks which was Crafers.

"Yes," he said reflectively, "I suppose I could."

The months, which were in his mind a row of unresolved emotions, began to string themselves together in a series of episodes, as if they had happened to someone else, and although no one told him, he knew that, just as he had written the Malayan jungle out of his system, so he could purge himself of Loveday in a book.

"It will be a long time before I try," he said at last.

"What are you going to do now?"

"After London I'm off to New York."

"About the book?"

"Partly. Doesn't it sound grand?"."

He grinned in artless pleasure.

"I won't be able to read your proofs."

She was filled with regret that all this interest was now to be taken away.

"If you really want to do them for me I'll send them to you."

"No, don't, there might be delays. It's too far."

New York seemed endlessly far away. Everyone was going there, Frances, Roberta, Ann. The size of it disappeared in her mind and she saw them all meeting as if they were in Overbridge High Street.

"How long will you stay?"

"Oh, I don't know. Till the cash runs out. I've got a restless feeling. I might work my way to Australia and see Mother."

He said no word of returning and Loveday felt as if a large world were taking him and swallowing him. The

347

caravan was untidy with the beginnings of his packing. He began to talk of practical things.

"I've asked Mrs. Spracker to clean the place up. Do you want any marg? I seem to have loads. Not doing any proper cooking, I suppose."

"When will you go to New York?"

"Depends. I've got to sell the car and scrape the money together for my fare. In a week or two, I suppose."

She had never understood his finances, which he had always described roughly as 'in the red'. She was surprised now to hear that he owned some stocks and shares and she was glad she had not made the mistake of offering to lend him some money, as she had often been tempted to do.

"You ought to find out where the Groves live in New York. They went back last week and took Ann back with them. You might be glad to see a familiar face over there."

He said loftily: "I've got friends there."

"Oh."

Once more she was aware of the stranger that he was, the stranger that he always had been.

"You can't resist, Loveday, throwing that awful Ann at me. I tell you that if she bores me in Overbridge she will bore me in New York. You know you've spoilt me for people like Ann."

"I'm sorry if I have, because she's an enchanting young thing, I've always thought. Anyone whose beauty could survive poodle-cuts and duffel coats must have something."

"Oh, I like the poodle-cut and the duffel coat. It's just the brashness of her I can't abide. I think perhaps our generation are swinging back to respectability."

"The smugness of you," cried Loveday.

"Yes, awful isn't it? And you and I have no right to be smug, have we?"

"None at all. No one has." She stood up and looked for her Wellingtons.

"I shall write to you sometimes," he added.

"Of course, I'll want to know all about the book."

"And about me?"

"And about you," she repeated.,

"There's something I want to tell you

349

about the book before you go. I'm going to dedicate it to you. Do you mind?"

"But my dear, of course I don't. What a charming idea."

"So you see," he went on, "when I send you a copy and you see on the dedication page 'For Loveday' you'll know it covers — everything — "

He spread out his hands in a helpless, weary gesture.

She let her feet drop and disappear into her Wellingtons, and in sober silence they walked together across the field. It was a grey day and there was a nip in the wind. She heard the beat of a swan's wings as it flew across the sky. The little gate was opened and closed and now stood between them.

"I'll come over and say 'Good-bye' tonight."

The farewells seemed endlessly protracted, thought Loveday, and she was glad to be able to say:

"But I shan't be here. It's the dress rehearsal of *Dear Octopus*."

"Gosh, is tonight the night? I'd forgotten. Lord, then I shan't see you again, Loveday. I've got to go to Hinwood and go to the bank and get my hair cut and old Martin, the bank manager, wants me to go and have a sherry with him, and I'll have to say 'Good-bye' to the Liverses and the Vicar. Loveday, this can't be good-bye here and now."

She smiled at his busy agitation. If he had a great deal to do he left it all to the last minute and then worked through it in panic-driven haste.

"It is good-bye, Peter, here and now."

"You've said the word. I shan't."

"But of course I hope I shall see you again one day and I shall always be interested to hear about you and to know of your success."

"I may be a failure."

"You won't. Success is a mixture of talent and a capacity for work, and I think you have both."

"It's nice to be believed in," he said with a grin, and, picking up her hand, he kissed it with the gentle politeness of a Frenchman.

"Gosh, Loveday, this isn't us. Give me a kiss, there's a good girl."

He dropped her hand, leant over the gate and kissed her with brotherly vigour.

That there was no passion in it surprised them both, and as they walked away, Loveday to Crafers and Peter to his caravan, each was a little oppressed at the transitoriness of what passes for love.

20

The Rehearsal

AT the Memorial Hall a state of confusion prevailed which only just fell short of chaos. On the stage, Mr. Gorman and his son Alf, who was alleged by his mother to be 'very clever at electricity', were arranging an ambitious but precarious form of lighting. Behind them Loveday was alarmed to find Mr. Fanshawe, who was only in the play at all because his wife willed it, was saying 'Ha Ha' to himself, in a vain endeavour to make a natural-sounding laugh. 'Ha *ha*,' said Mr. Fanshaw, occasionally varying the emphasis to '*Ha* ha' or multiplying it to 'Ha Ha *Ha*.'

Behind a screen the piano tuner was at work, for the Memorial Hall was so damp that the piano had to be tuned immediately before the show, and into the general hubbub came an intermittent off-key 'pang'.

"When I first came here," said Marcy, who was pinning up the hem of Fenny's dress in a corner, "we used to take the whole of the inside out and warm it at Friar's House before it would work at all."

Her voice plainly showed, in spite of the peril of swallowing pins, that she thought such refinements as preferring the piano to be in tune to be a sign of an effete modern generation.

Mr. Finch from the Duke's Head was arranging chairs and forms on the floor of the hall and the girl for whom Loveday was playing the piano was looking wildly for her music,

"I've got it," said Loveday calmly. "Don't you remember I said I would take it home with me?"

"I don't remember anything," said the girl. "I don't remember any part or the song or anything, and what I'd like most of all would be to break my leg here and now. I haven't slept a wink."

An art student who happened to be staying with the Lambes had painted the scenery, which was remarkably good.

With boxes and a painted back cloth he had contrived a life-like dummy piano, on which the singer would accompany herself, while Loveday, a foot away behind the scenery, was to play, assisted in timing by Mrs. Fanshawe's Michael, aged thirteen, who co-ordinated the performance by glueing his eye cunningly to a hole in the backcloth and poking Loveday with a walking-stick. There was much that could and did go wrong with this system and 'Cynthia' had every reason to be nervous, but at the sight of her panic Loveday became completely calm and suggested cups of tea all round.

Everyone knew where the key to the cupboard was kept, but there was no tea and no milk and no one had a shilling for the gas. Mrs. Wales, who lived opposite the Memorial Hall, and whose house was therefore used as a kind of annexe where people dumped keys and fetched books and borrowed trays, volunteered to stop decorating the sides of the stage with a gloomy erection of artificial flowers and fir branches over from the Parish Social party, and go home to make tea for everyone. In expectation of this the tuner proclaimed his job to be done by executing a clever series of runs up and down the piano, ending with a short excerpt from Chopin's *Ballade* in A Minor. Mr. Fanshawe gave a final and exhausted 'Ha ha,' and Cynthia put off having hysterics.

★ ★ ★

Before Loveday could have believe it possible an hour had gone and now the dress rehearsal proper was due to start. The audience consisted of the wardrobe mistress, otherwise Marcy, Mrs. Fanshawe's eldest, Mr. Gorman and Alf, and Loveday, whose appearance was short in Act II. They sat in lonely splendour in the front row.

There was a certain amount of coming and going at the back and the prompter was very overworked. As at many dress rehearsals, the effect was worse than one would have thought possible, and, by the end, everyone, except Mrs. Fanshawe, who, Loveday felt, would not be downcast by battle, murder or sudden death, was depressed in various degrees. Even Mr.

Fanshawe no longer attempted to put joviality into his 'Ha ha.' Marcy said without conviction that she supposed it would be all right on the night.

Loveday was the only member of the company who lived on the top of the hill and she was offered lifts by Mrs. Fanshawe and Marcy's husband, who was waiting patiently outside, but she thanked them and said that she would rather walk.

"But you can't walk," said Marcy, squeezing herself backwards into their small Ford.

Those who lived at the bottom of the hill seldom walked to the top. For centuries all their interests had spread away along the valley; there were a few new bungalows as the road left the village and wound towards the Livers' farm, which ended as a seldom used track through the woods. On the other side the hill dropped slowly into Lower Spedding, which was three miles away and in another world.

"I really would like to walk," said Loveday. "I feel full of Memorial Hall fug and I'm used to the climb."

This was true for she now found she had muscles never before used and the hill worried her no more than it had all the former people who had lived at Crafers. She thought of Miss Cox, who had, it seemed, walked down to Overbridge and back every week to collect her pension until three days before she died at the age of ninety-five.

She said 'Good-night' and heard the cars roar away along the main road. Mr. Gorman disappeared into his yard by the church. 'Fenny', whose real name Loveday never discovered and who remained to the end 'the girl in the Post Office', walked with Loveday up the street.

"Were we terrible, do you think?" she asked timidly.

"You weren't, my dear," said Loveday truthfully, for indeed 'Fenny' had revealed considerable and surprising talent, "but the others were a bit grim. I suppose most village shows are put on for the fun of the performers rather than the audience."

'Fenny' considered this idea and said no more until she turned down the road above Friar's House with a friendly 'Good-night'.

Loveday plodded on up the hill, which sloped gently for the first quarter of a mile and was lit by the windows of the last houses of Overbridge, a straggling collection which stopped where the hill suddenly became very steep and justified the ominous signs at the bottom: 'Dangerous Hill. 1 in 4.' There was a seat here and another at the top, which at this time of night were usually occupied by loving couples hidden in the friendly dark, so that Loveday could not rest, as she generally did in the daytime, to regain her breath and enjoy the view.

She was not frightened by the dark, for nothing, she decided, could ever be so terrifying as London in the blackout, and she was surprised how few countrywomen would walk alone after nightfall. She heard the owls screeching across the woods and the sudden roar of a motor bicycle, but the winding hill was not favoured by much traffic, which could now avoid it on the new by-pass. At the top she drew a deep breath and felt the sudden ease of walking on level ground. She quickened her pace and was soon turning down the lane to Crafers, a swift glance across the field telling her that Peter and his car had gone. There was a dark shape in the corner, which was the caravan waiting for its occupation by the 'sensible Sellinges'.

She undid the back door and let air into the stuffy house. All life seemed to have left it. On the mat lay a wisp of paper, a scribbled note from Peter.

I found I had all sorts of bits of food over so I put them in your shed. Give them to Mrs. Spracker if you don't want them. You see, I'm romantic to the last!

Yours as always but with a difference
Peter.

She stood reading the note over and over, her heart beating in her throat. Then she put the chain on the door and made herself a cup of Ovaltine. By the time she was in bed she decided that the bleakness which enveloped her would be gone by morning, but it was a long time before she slept.

360

21

Piper's Tune

OUT of sight Loveday struck a chord and the audience who had sat through *Dear Octopus*, as performed by the Overbridge Players, shuffled to its feet for the National Anthem. She couldn't believe that it was all over, the rehearsals, the worry, and, she was forced to admit, the fun. The excited cast were all weighed down with workmanlike bouquets, made by Mr. State, the local nurseryman and florist. Even Loveday and Michael Fanshawe had been dragged out from their hiding-place and given buttonholes. She never discovered who gave what to whom, but she supposed that the odd sixpences which had been taken from the players from time to time had paid for them.

The finances of the show appalled Loveday, for Mr. Gorman, who was also, it seemed, the Treasurer of everything, had whispered to Loveday that they had made six pounds, ten shillings and twopence profit, and he was, moreover, so obviously pleased that Loveday bit her tongue on the words: 'Is that all?' It seemed so little reward for so much effort, but when the royalties, the hire of the hall, the printing and other sundry expenses were taken away, six pounds, ten shillings and twopence remained. If pressed, Loveday could have given them the sum without much self-denial and saved herself time and trouble. Then she looked along at the cast and realized this was their moment which money could not buy. Even Mr. Fanshawe, whose features were not without distinction, when he was saying 'Ha-ha' had a fleeting likeness to Sir Lawrence Olivier. The stage make-up had so improved the women, except 'Fenny', who had somewhat overdone the eyeblack, that Loveday felt when she saw them next day with their baskets in Church Street she would hardly recognize them.

She looked along the front rows of the audience at a line of faces, if not known, at any rate familiar, and she would not admit that her eyes were searching for Julian, or that she was disappointed when she did not see anyone from Friar's House.

Mrs. Fanshawe had asked her to Vane End to an After the Show party and she had made excuses, being sure that it would be much more fun at Friar's House, and there was bound to be a party there, for the household was a party in itself. She pictured Ann arguing with Frances and Johnny's pointed face and Roberta's square one. She saw Marcy dispensing coffee and Julian's thin face a mixture of despair and exhaustion and at the same time the hub of it all. Suddenly she realized that the people went to Friar's House not, as Julian so often deplored, because it was the centre of Overbridge or even because it was convenient. There were two other houses nearby which would have done equally well.

It was the master of Friar's House which gave it something which Miss Drake of No. 5 Church Street and Tom Hove on the corner did not possess. It was Julian who left the door ajar,

Julian who gave the drinks, Julian who asked the wayfarer in, and Julian who complained so bitterly when his shabby, friendly, awkward house was always full.

The thought that there would be no After the Show party at Friar's House depressed Loveday and when the curtain came down at last she picked up her music, and shut the piano with sad finality. The jingle of 'Kerry Dancers' tinkled in her brain as if it were a musical box. It was so mournful that she felt as dismal as the actors in the play in the Nursery Scene. She gave herself a shake: 'Now is your own curtain,' she said to herself. 'Pull it down and go home,' and with hardly a farewell to the over-excited company she slipped out with the audience.

"Oh, there you are," said Marcy on the steps of the Memorial Hall. "I made sure you'd be going to the Fanshawes! I told Julian so. I got out of it myself. Mind you, I'd have enjoyed it. I dearly love anything I haven't arranged myself, but it's a dangerous thing to put Jack in the same room as Robert Fanshawe because his dog will chase our sheep. And anyhow

I can't help feeling sorry for Julian."

"Why? Is he ill?"

"They've all gone," she said. There was such gloom in her voice that Loveday heard it echoing round the emptiness of Friar's House.

"Didn't you know?" she went on. "Landon flew back a fortnight ago and Frances took Ann and Roberta on Friday. It was Johnny's half-term and Julian took him back this evening. That's why he didn't come to the play. Johnny had to be there by six and Julian had a client to see at Avonbury Spa and he said he was having dinner at that place at Foxhurst on the way home. Do you know it?"

Loveday said that she did, something prevented her from telling Marcy that Julian had taken her there earlier in the year. On looking back it seemed worlds away. Marcy's husband drove them slowly up the street from the Memorial Hall. For such a short distance it hardly seemed worth the effort of getting in and out. Since her marriage Marcy continued to gain weight, and though she talked of dieting, she lived too well and was too happy to persecute herself. Now she had reached the stage of treating her size as a joke. As she left the car she went on talking, interrupted by puffs and sighs.

"He'll miss them all, you know. Of course he grumbled but he will rattle about in that old place. I hate to think of him being there all alone, but Frances has found him a married couple. She interviewed them in London, so I don't know what they are like."

She sounded as if she had no faith in the judgement of Frances.

"When do they come?"

"Next month."

She opened the door by turning its round brass knob and called; "Julian. Julian."

At first there was no answer and Marcy walked on down the passage. Loveday stood hesitant on the mat. At last Julian came out of his study, half-asleep, paper in hand, his voice gruff with pleasure.

"Good heavens, Marcy, is the place on fire? What a row to kick up. I was nearly asleep."

Marcy's bulk hid Loveday at first, but when Julian saw her he became more polite and asked courteously about the play.

"If I made some coffee, Julian," Marcy asked, "may we have some?"

"Yes, if there is any coffee."

Marcy walked through the familiar doors to the kitchen. Jack Lowesmore decided he would put the car in the yard of the Duke's Head to save his lights, and for a moment Loveday and Julian were alone.

He stood by the mantelpiece fiddling with an empty cartridge which was amongst the clutter there of piled up ashtrays, pipe cleaners, Chelsea figures and a home-made calendar.

"Was Johnny all right?" asked Loveday.

"Perfectly. He seems very happy," said Julian. "I was the one who nearly disgraced himself. He looked so wan and pathetic in that horrible blazer and cap. I felt I was throwing him to the wolves. I don't believe I was ever so unhappy as when I went back to school, but I daresay kids are more sensible nowadays."

"Or the schools are better."

"Yes, maybe, when I talk about my schooldays it all sounds like Dotheboys

Hall. I can't get over the feeling that it's unnatural to like school, but they seem to nowadays. I expect he's all right." He turned his back to her and blew his nose. She saw the shininess of his best blue suit which he had worn to impress the Headmaster, and she had noticed that his tie did not match and that a hole was beginning over his heel. He had a moment of pathos which made him resemble his son lost in his new red blazer.

Marcy came in, complaining that the coffee was stale and the biscuits soft. Jack Lowesmore appeared and, in his usual manner, filled up space in the room, while adding nothing to the conversation. Marcy wanted to know about Frances's departure and whether Ann had had time to make the damson jam before she went and, in her shabby chair, Loveday leaned back and wondered why this room had become the distilled essence of Overbridge to her. She supposed it was some quality of life and permanence which it possessed. Although Marcy and Frances talked of making Julian leave it, she did not believe they would succeed.

"I'll take Miss Flayne up the hill," said Julian, when Marcy and her husband rose to go. "It's not on your route and I haven't put the car away."

Jack said it was no trouble and Loveday made the usual protests of the car-less.

"I must try and scrape together enough to buy a car this winter," she said. "I'm nothing but an eternal nuisance to my friends."

"Don't be silly," said Marcy. "You can always get a lift. Well, Julian, perhaps we'll be going then." She gave them both what can only be expressed as 'a look' and Loveday felt acutely uncomfortable, as if there were something licentious at being left with Julian at such a late hour.

He shut the door on the Lowesmores and she stood waiting for him to fetch his car.

"Don't go," he said. "I never have a chance to talk to you and I've wanted to apologize for the other evening. I realize I didn't give you a chance, but Frances said — "

Loveday interrupted him with an amused smile.

"So it was your sister's idea?"

He was standing at the other end of the fireplace, ill at ease. A log fell forward and Loveday bent down quickly to save the rug. She noticed that it was covered in small burns merged in the Persian pattern.

"Frances thought I ought to be married," he admitted.

"And so she thought I would do," added Loveday. She felt her seldom-roused temper rising.

"It wasn't that exactly. You're making a mistake," said Julian. "It — it wasn't at all like that."

She was still on the rug making the fire safe, and she could not see his face.

"It's just," went on Julian looking at the nape of her neck and noticing for the first time the grey hairs in each curl, "that I like you so much I should be most unhappy if I thought my tactlessness had stopped us from being friends. When I thought about it afterwards I realized how badly I'd managed the whole thing, and Frances said — "

Loveday sat back on her heels wielding the poker. "To hell with Frances," she said. "No, I'm not going to attack you, though I'd like to. Really, Julian, don't you know anything about women?"

"Not much," he admitted. He sat down on a fireside stool and put his head in his hands, and again she thought of Johnny.

"Take me home, my dear," she said gently.

He did not move. It seemed as if he had not heard. Then he looked at her with his misleadingly fierce gaze.

"Loveday, don't go."

She put out her hand and stroked his. "Dear Julian," she said. "I must go. I know you only want to talk and I sound just like Mrs. Livers, but think what people will say. It's awfully late. There's the question of my fair name."

It was the first time she had ever been in Friar's House without at least four people and it had for a moment a hunted feeling as if its laughing ghosts lingered.

As if he saw into her mind he said: "I'm so lonely."

She thought again that there was something forlorn about him, like a forsaken child, but she smiled and said: "I expect you'll get used to it. I did. And think how you used to complain."

He made an impatient gesture. "Any moment you'll be saying 'I told you so'."

She picked up the cups and said: "I'll wash these up for you before I go," and despite protests she carried them into the kitchen. She had never been into the kitchen of Friar's House before and she was aghast at its size. The whole of the ground floor of Crafers would have fitted into it. In spite of the modern embellishments of the Aga Cooker, it remained inconvenient, and Frances had longed all the summer to tear it apart. There was, however, a certain cosiness about it. The light shone on the blue china and the red tins and its untidiness was lost in its size. Moreover, it was warm with an enclosed smell compounded of all the cooking ever done down the centuries.

On one side of the fireplace there was a dog, on the other side a cat, who had stirred at their entrance and then relaxed into sleep.

She washed up the cups and saucers and Julian, out of habit, picked up a tea-cloth and dried them.

As he put away the china on the dresser she hung the towel on a rail, standing for a moment on tiptoe with her arms raised, for it was too high for her. Afterwards, Julian could not have explained the suddenness of his desire of her, mixed with a misplaced feeling that she was a small defenceless thing whom he must protect. It struck him with an abruptness which he did not expect, and he found that he was trembling. He helped her into her coat, disturbed with longing by the touch of her shoulders. Together in silence they went outside to the car. There was one light upstairs where Mrs. Duke's Head was putting curlers in her hair, and there was no sound but their footsteps on the cobbles, and the banging of the old stable door. They were in the car now. It started after the usual preliminary struggle and they moved out into the street and up the hill, along Crafers Lane.

He found her torch and opened the car door for her. The gate clicked, the garden looked frozen in moonlight.

Loveday knew that Julian would kiss her. She knew what he was going to say, and when she saw Crafers looking at her like an empty box, with a rush of happiness she knew what her answer would be.

THE END

Other titles in the Ulverscroft Large Print Series:

TO FIGHT THE WILD
Rod Ansell and Rachel Percy

Lost in uncharted Australian bush, Rod Ansell survived by hunting and trapping wild animals, improvising shelter and using all the bushman's skills he knew.

COROMANDEL
Pat Barr

India in the 1830s is a hot, uncomfortable place, where the East India Company still rules. Amelia and her new husband find themselves caught up in the animosities which seethe between the old order and the new.

THE SMALL PARTY
Lillian Beckwith

A frightening journey to safety begins for Ruth and her small party as their island is caught up in the dangers of armed insurrection.

THE WILDERNESS WALK
Sheila Bishop

Stifling unpleasant memories of a misbegotten romance in Cleave with Lord Francis Aubrey, Lavinia goes on holiday there with her sister. The two women are thrust into a romantic intrigue involving none other than Lord Francis.

THE RELUCTANT GUEST
Rosalind Brett

Ann Calvert went to spend a month on a South African farm with Theo Borland and his sister. They both proved to be different from her first idea of them, and there was Storr Peterson — the most disturbing man she had ever met.

ONE ENCHANTED SUMMER
Anne Tedlock Brooks

A tale of mystery and romance and a girl who found both during one enchanted summer.